Here's what critics are saying about Sally J. Smith & Jean Steffens's books:

"A great series and smart plot told at breakneck pace...great characters, sexy, tough, intelligent, and witty....the perfect companion for the beach, planes, trains and everything else in between."
—*The New York Journal of Books*

"Smart and sassy. Classy with a twist of wry humor and just enough sentiment and romance to reel you in and keep you hanging until the end. Smith and Steffens, partners in crime, have struck gold.
—Kathleen M. Rodgers, author of *Johnnie Come Lately* and *The Final Salute*

"Stealing the Moon & Stars is an impossible book to put down. Jordan and Eddie are the best mystery solving duo since Nick and Nora. Is there a fire alarm ringing? Because their relationship is smokin' hot!"
—Jenn McKinlay, *New York Times* bestselling author of the Cupcake Bakery Mysteries and the Library Lover's Mysteries

"The action and sexual tension are as hot as an Arizona summer. The Shea Investigations team put their lives, and their hearts, on the line in this action-packed crime novel."
—*Lesa's Book Critiques*

"This mystery unfolds with humorous zingers. Tingling with sexual tension, this is a satisfying read. I highly recommend it!"
—Nancy Redd, author of *The Canyon's Edge*

BOOKS BY
SALLY J. SMITH & JEAN STEFFENS

MYSTIC MAYHEM

a Mystic Isle mystery

Sally J. Smith &
Jean Steffens

We'd like to thank Ryan Durkee, tattoo artist extraordinaire, for consenting to be our go-to guy for the thousands of questions regarding any and all things tattoo-related for the entire Mystic Isle series. Thanks, Ryan, you rock!
http://www.eyeconicart.com

And we're sending off a special shout-out to Janet Holmes, cover artist extraordinaire, who's not only patient and thorough, but she also absolutely *crushed* our cover art. Loads of appreciation and admiration to you, Janet.

Such generous and talented people we're privileged to work with.

—Sally & Jean

CHAPTER ONE

───

I was making short work of an order of beignets and well into my coffee, the caffeine just kicking in, when my best friend and roomie, Catalina Gabor, finally showed up at the Café du Monde in New Orleans' French Quarter.

"Sorry I'm late, Mel."

I looked up at her and stifled a yawn. "No problem. You're still in time to catch the ferry." I handed her the last warm sugar-powdered beignet. I'd eaten the rest of the order. She was late, and the way I looked at it, she was lucky there was even one left. She tapped the pastry against the side of the plate and knocked off half the powder. It kept her from wearing the sugar on her chest like I sometimes did.

She took a couple of bites and laid the rest of the beignet aside. I made a mental note to myself: *Chère, you should try that one too.*

Myself replied*: But, chère, they're too good to leave on the plate.*

"You look tired, Mel," Cat said. "I bet you worked all weekend at the church."

"I did. Putting in some long hours over there, hoping to have it ready for services by Thanksgiving."

The Lower Ninth Ward and Holy Cross neighborhoods east of the city were hit so hard by Katrina, even a decade later they looked like war zones. Churches, schools, and even fire stations were still boarded up and crumbling away. Federal funds went to the more prosperous, commercial neighborhoods of the Crescent City area, so it was left up to the citizenry, all the king's horses and all the king's men, *moi,* and people like me to mobilize and put St. Antoine's Parish back together again.

My heart lies there. It's my old stomping grounds where Mama and I lived until Grandmama Ida took us in. It's where many of my childhood friends still live. It's where I put any extra money I'm lucky enough to come across and as many extra hours that happen to turn up in my day.

The chapel of St. Antoine's Parish, deconsecrated after Katrina due to brutal damage, was being revived due to the generosity of a celebrity musician who grew up in the area. His money, together with the money and efforts of some of us less celebrated New Orleans folk, was bringing back the simple beauty and sense of community to St. Antoine's. That week I'd spent my days off—eight hours on Thursday and ten hours on Friday—helping put up new siding. Now it was Saturday morning, time to go back to my paying job, and my arms, legs, and back testified to all my hard labor. But I loved every minute of it. And that lovely old church? Why, she was coming back around.

Cat laid her hand on mine. "Melanie Hamilton, girl, you're racking up points in Heaven. And that's the blessed truth." She reached slim fingers with purple-lacquered nails across the table, snagged my coffee cup, and took a swig of the dark, heavy chicory that was both our addictions. We like it *regulah*, lots of cream, tons of sugar.

I looked at my watch—10:50 a.m.—and stood. "We better get a move on."

She fell in step beside me as we double-timed it along the riverfront walkway to where the dedicated ferryboat for The Mansion at Mystic Isle bobbed against the old-fashioned wooden dock. We jumped onto the brightly painted flat-bottom boat with a few minutes to spare.

George, the ferry conductor, swept off his Mystic Isle cap, offered a toothy smile, and gave us an exaggerated bow. "Miss Hamilton," he drawled. "Miss Gabor. Glorious mornin', ladies. Dat f'sure."

Mid-July. It wasn't noon yet, and the temp had already climbed to the high eighties. There wasn't even the slightest breeze, and the humidity was no less than killer. You almost had to pull the air apart like a curtain just to walk through it. Yep, a glorious day, all right. My T-shirt clung to me like wet wallpaper. The light complexion that went along with my strawberry-blonde hair wasn't ideal for life in a place where the sun beat down like my own personal heat lamp. I was thankful for the ferry's canopy.

While I was sweating like a hooker in a front-row church pew, Catalina bestowed a smile on George that was cool as a spring mist over a clear lake. No wonder he was nuts about her.

The only other passengers were a few of the dinner kitchen staff and the hotel's voodoo priestess (her *official* title) who ran the Who-do Voodoo We-do Shop at The Mansion.

The Mansion at Mystic Isle was where Cat and I worked. Located in Jefferson Parish across the Mississippi from New Orleans at the edge of a bayou, the main building was an old plantation house set among cypress trees and expansive green lawns. It had been handed down through the Villars family for centuries. Not all that long ago, Harry Villars, the down-on-his-luck, but no less genteel and stylish owner, had the brilliant idea to turn his liability into an asset by repurposing the place into a resort where folks dedicated to the supernatural and all kinds of magic could come and get their creep on.

The Mansion was decorated like the haunted house we've all seen at that theme park—you know the one. Ours was similar—creepy organ music when you crossed the threshold, drafty hallways, creaky doors, secret passages, even fake cobwebs. The whole shebang, *chère*. Harry Villars sank every cent he had into it and crossed his fingers that the place would raise him to the ranks of the solvent—then he hired all of us, a complete cast of soothsayers and charlatans, to convince hotel guests the supernatural stuff that went on at The Mansion was the real deal. But just between you, me, and the gators, it's not.

Cat was the gypsy fortune-teller, and did she ever look the part. Flashing dark eyes, long, flowing locks the color of cappuccino. Her lips always looked as if they were stained persimmon without any lip-gloss, and her size Ds were nothing short of a masterpiece. When she left our apartment in the French Quarter to head to work, she dressed like any regular twenty-eight-year-old knockout, but once her shift began at the resort, she was decked out in layers of gauzy jewel tones and bling, lots and lots of bling.

Me? I was the designated artist at The Mansion's Dragons and Deities Tattoo Parlor. My work costume was a slinky black gown with a V-neck, empire waist, and a big stand-up collar that fanned all the way around the back of my neck from one collar bone to the other. I think the effect was intended to be darkly glamorous, but most days I felt more like the Count von Count Muppet than Elvira, Mistress of the Dark. I would have preferred that free and easy Stevie Nicks look Cat pulled off, but it wasn't in the cards—not when I was forced to wear a full bib apron on top of that gorgeous creation to avoid spraying ink all over it.

When I walked out of college with my degree in fine arts, I never would have suspected tattoos would be my groceries, and I still don't consider myself to be your typical tattoo girl. No leather bustier or nose ring, and the only tattoo on this girl's milky skin is a tiny Tinker Bell on my right shoulder.

The boat motor revved. The signal horn blew, and the ferry pulled out into the strong draft of the mighty Mississippi River, brown as liquid chocolate and churning like a whirlpool. Cat and I leaned against the railing, shoulder to shoulder, and I turned my face into the wind created by the movement of the boat. It cooled me off a little.

"You look nice today," Cat said.

Oh. My makeup must not have been running down my face like melting Häagen-Dazs yet. "Thanks, Cat. So do you."

"Well," she said without the slightest bit of arrogance, "I look nice every day."

I nodded. *When you're right, you're right.*

"You hoping to run into Cap'n Jack, girl?" Her voice was sly.

I bumped her shoulder with mine. "You pokin' fun at me?" It was true. I had taken extra care with my makeup and hair that morning. Some VIPs were checking in at Mystic Isle today, and I knew the manager, Jack Stockton, would be up front and present to take care of them.

"Poking fun at you? No, girl, no way. Settin' your cap for a man like that is some serious stuff."

A man like that.

Jack Stockton—Cat and I had taken to calling him Cap'n Jack—was the recently hired general manager at The Mansion on Mystic Isle. The story was he had been the golden boy moving up the corporate ladder at an international chain's premier property in the Big Apple when disaster struck. The hotel chain's CEO had arrived in New York from Frankfurt for a look-see at his crown jewel. The grapevine rumored that Jack Stockton met a stunning blonde with a provocative Marlene Dietrich accent at the hotel lounge. The two hit off and wound up back at his place. The next morning Jack discovered the blonde was the boss's twenty-five-year-old bride of only six weeks. They didn't even let him clean out his desk, and once the story got around, poor Jack couldn't even walk into a hotel without turning every head in the place. At least in the Big Apple.

But New York was a far cry from the Big Easy.

The Mansion at Mystic Isle was just getting a foothold, and the idea of having a man as capable yet desperate for work as Jack Stockton sat just right with Harry Villars, who needed someone with monster talent to manage his supernatural resort project. The weird goings-on, unusual clientele, bizarre employees, and rumors of hauntings at our beloved place of employment had already driven off three general managers. I had high hopes for Jack.

He was smart, experienced, and would probably do whatever it took to make the place a success. And besides, Harry Villars was gay. It wasn't likely Jack would get caught in bed with Harry's significant other, my good friend the Great Fabrizio. Still, Jack would need every bit of skill and cunning he could muster to get this albatross on solid ground. I think I fell in love with him the first time he lifted that chiseled chin and showed me that smile.

Saying Cap'n Jack was easy on the eyes was an understatement of Biblical proportion. Dark eyes, slightly almond-shaped. Smooth, swarthy skin. Full lips that slid easily into a lopsided sexy smile and short, dark hair my fingers itched to lace themselves into. The Fifth Avenue suits he wore to work every day appeared tailor-made to fit his athletic body but still somehow looked out of place on him. My mind's eye insisted on imagining him in boots, jeans, and muscle shirts. And when he came to me in my dreams, he wore a lot less.

He was a really nice guy whose New York ways made him a duck in the desert among the laid-back, slow-talking New Orleanians, Cajuns, and swamp rats at Mystic Isle.

On his first day at The Mansion Jack stood in front of the entire staff and told his tale about the consequences of looking for love in all the wrong places. He made sure we laughed at what had to be a difficult and embarrassing incident in his life and made us all as comfortable with him as he was with himself. Honesty and good humor were just about the two sexiest traits a man could have. And Jack had both—in spades.

Don't get me wrong. I liked his sophisticated style, so much that whenever he even walked into the room, I came apart like a house of cards in a wind tunnel. At least that was how I felt. He made me warm and cold, excited and nervous, happy and scared all at the same time.

I think he might have been interested in me, too, but I couldn't be sure he didn't think I was the village idiot, not the way my tongue tangled itself up whenever I tried to speak to him.

Cat, God love her, was still trying her best to hook us up.

Despite her efforts, it wasn't likely to happen. He was kind and fair and had a great laugh, but he was also my boss. I didn't figure either of us was ready to risk the livelihood of the other, so I went home every night and carried on a steamy love affair with him in my dreams.

"I'm just sayin', *chère*," Cat closed her eyes and lifted her face to the breeze coming off the river, "dat man is delish, fo' true."

I glanced sideways at her, slid my hand along the railing, and laid it on top of hers. "And I'm just sayin', *chère,* you're spending too much time with that Cajun cop of yours. And dat f'shore too."

* * *

Once we docked, the ride to the resort on Mystic Isle took thirty minutes if there weren't any gators sunbathing in the road or big mud holes that had to be skirted. The shuttle ran back and forth all day every day from seven a.m. until midnight. It was a sight to behold, basically a smallish airport shuttle only N'awlins style. The front end was a purple Mardi Gras mask with headlights serving as eyes. On either side, The Mansion at Mystic Isle was scrolled in gold letters over dark but beautifully screened images glimpsing into the paranormal world of spirits and spells. Its route went via Jefferson Parish into the swamplands near the Barataria Preserve then over the bridge to the privately owned four square miles of swampland that was now the country's first, and possibly only, resort catering to those who believed in all things mystical and occult.

I stepped down from the shuttle just as Jack Stockton jogged up, out of breath, and spicier than Louisiana hot sauce.

"You need to turn around," he told the driver. "The Elway woman and her people are on their way from the airport to the ferry. If you're not there to pick them up, it won't be good."

As the shuttle circled back out, Jack turned and seemed to see me for the first time.

"Good morning, Miss Hamilton," he said quickly. That was just one of the things that set him apart from the locals. You never heard "Where y'at, baaay-beee?" or "Aw right, dawlin'" from his gorgeous lips. No sir, always polite and cultured, my Jack. My Jack? My fervent wish.

He wasn't in such a big hurry that he didn't take the time to notice. "Miss Hamilton, I believe that shirt just exactly matches your green eyes." Interest flared in his gorgeous peepers.

I smiled but didn't answer. As flummoxed as I was, it would have sounded like a foreign language.

After the shuttle turned back around, so did Jack. He stopped at the front entrance, and while the organ music groaned the welcome dirge, he asked Lurch, our obsessed-by-selfies doorman, how his day was going, and then he said to the morose giant of a man, "There are some VIP guests arriving later today. I'm going to request, as a personal favor to me, you not ask them to join you for a selfie. Please."

The fact that Lurch asked anyone and everyone to pose for a selfie with him seemed to bother Jack—the uptight New

Yorker in him, I supposed. None of the rest of us cared a whit about it. In fact, it was a lot of fun to sit down with Lurch on a coffee break and have a slide show of all the pictures on his phone.

It didn't hurt anybody, and if someone didn't want to stand beside a seven-foot-tall, pasty-skinned man with hands the size of cast-iron skillets, they could always say, "No thanks."

Lurch groaned but nodded. "Yes, sir."

* * *

The Dragons and Deities Tattoo Parlor was located on the first floor of the auxiliary wing next to the hotel spa. The hotel owner, Harry Villars, a genteel Southern man with grand gestures and the soft-spoken mannerisms of Ashley Wilkes, had pretty much given me carte blanche in decorating, and I went with the Medieval Times look. Since the name of the place had to do with dungeons, it was just about my only reference material. The flickering wall sconces, stone masonry wallpaper, and red and gold drapery swags were nothing if not dramatic.

I was not ashamed to admit I kind of got off on wearing that girly garb the mystical theme required, and the skin paintings I created are ethereal and otherworldly. They went hand-in-hand with the theme of the hotel and more often than not challenged my artistic nature.

My first love was oil on canvas. The streets and people of New Orleans, my favorite subjects. When I didn't spend my weekend working at St. Antoine's trying to bring the beautiful old church back, I hauled myself out to Jackson Square and displayed my wares with other struggling artists. A gallery over on Julia Street took the odd painting every now and then. When I sold one, what I got for it went straight to the neighborhood restoration fund.

It was about three o'clock. My last client of the day, a nerdy neurosurgeon from Wisconsin, was still in the chair, just getting up from my work on the wizard I'd inked on his left butt cheek. He'd been all worried someone would see it, so he asked me to put it there, folks. It wasn't my idea. Believe me. The finished product was pretty gorgeous, if I do say so myself. The wizard's light-blue flowing beard, royal-blue flowing robes, and pointy hat were offset with the red sparks that flew from his wand. I had to say it kind of made me grumpy no one would ever see it. But like they say, the customer is always right. If he wanted a tattoo on his butt, who was I to deny him?

He'd just walked out when Catalina and Cap'n Jack walked into my domain.

Jack cleared his throat. "Miss Hamilton…"

"This is the South, Mr. Stockton," I said. "Please call me Mel."

His eyes found mine. "And I'm Jack," he said.

Cap'n Jack—it was all I could do not to say it out loud.

He went on. "I've already asked Miss Gabor—Catalina—but I wanted to ask you personally. Mrs. Elway and her party have arrived a day early. We can accommodate her with rooms, thank God, but the dining room is booked tonight for the annual banquet of the Dead-and-Loving-It Zombie Fan Club. I've arranged for Mrs. Elway and her guests to be served in the small dining room, but it's too late to bring in extra waitstaff from the city to serve them. I know it's not your job, and ordinarily I wouldn't ask, but I'm sure you've heard Cecile Elway and her personal psychic, Penelope Devere, are the president and vice-president of the International Paranormal Society. Their endorsement will put The Mansion on the map." He paused as those eyes and lips pleaded his case for him. I tried to concentrate on what he was actually saying. He was so, as Cat would say, *delish*. "It's a small group," he went on, "just six of them including the Great Fabrizio."

"She's having dinner with the hotel medium?"

"Yep." He shook his head as if the idea amazed him. "That's why she's here. Her personal psychic told Cecile to come. Said Theodore Elway, Cecile's deceased husband, spoke to her in a dream and wanted Mrs. Elway to have a séance with the Great Fabrizio to learn the secret to her husband's restless soul finding peace." He shook his head. "You know, if you'd asked me six months ago if I'd be lining up ghostly encounters for hotel guests, I'd have laughed you out of the room." He raised his eyes to mine. "And just look at me now, begging you to help me do this ridiculous thing."

I tried to ignore the amber gleam in his eyes. *Keep it business, Mel. He is.* "I'll do anything I can to help out. Just tell me what you need."

* * *

I offered my last scheduled appointment of the day a really nice discount to reschedule her body art, the Gryffindor crest from Harry Potter targeted for her right calf, and closed the parlor early. After changing into the proper uniforms, typical black-and-white antebellum-style long dresses and aprons, Cat and I took a crash course in table service lessons from the main dining room maître d'.

The smaller dining room was furnished with lovely period furniture that could well have been used in The Mansion during its plantation days in the 1800s. The oval table seated up to ten people. Mrs. Elway and the other five guests were comfortable that evening.

The widow was Cecile Elway, a fifty-something aristocratic-looking dishwater blonde with blue eyes, a strong chin, and aquiline nose she kept so high in the air I was pretty sure she had a stiff neck from it. She was haughtily lovely for (who my mama would call) a woman of that certain age.

Her stepdaughter, Rosalyn Elway Whitlock, on the other hand, looked like a small-town librarian with poodle-cut curly hair, watery grey eyes, face scrubbed so clean it shone, and a brown suit jacket over a white blouse buttoned all the way to the collar. A pair of tortoiseshell reading glasses dangled on a beaded chain around her neck. Her head stayed down, and her eyes stayed glued to the place setting in front of her.

Elway's stepgrandson, Billy Whitlock, was college-aged from the look of him, probably still had to have his nose wiped by his mama. He was skinny with an Adam's apple that sat in the middle of his throat like a golf ball. He only smiled at me, but when Cat walked by he jumped to his feet, took hold of her hand, and made a big deal about kissing it. I was surprised she didn't run into the kitchen and grab a bar of soap.

Then there was Terrence Montague. He was introduced as the President of the Society for the Preservation of the

Lepidoptera Alien Caterpillar (say that fast three times). There was something about his smarmy good looks I didn't like. The Buddy Holly glasses didn't fit his persona. The fuzzy caterpillar pin on his lapel looked like it might have been solid gold, but it was as out of place on him as a My Little Pony T-shirt would have looked on me. Beside him, Cecile had her hand on his thigh.

Mrs. Elway's personal psychic, Penelope Devere, was there too. She was a short woman built like a fireplug. She might have been cute at one time, but today's look, the Little Dutch Boy haircut and her plain unmade-up features, didn't do much to add to her mystique.

Last, but no way least, was Fabrizio, the hotel's resident medium and a person dear to my heart, also known as the Great Fabrizio. He was one of my favorite people on the planet. Born in Yorkshire across the pond, he grew up poor, as he said, "With little more than a pence or two in the pocket of the hand-me-down trousers from my older brother. Fancied myself a bit of an Oliver Twist." He was about as much a psychic medium as I was the Dalai Lama.

Talk around the hotel was, back in the salad days he'd been honored by the Queen for his performances as Macbeth and Hamlet. There was little trace of that left in him these days. Formally trained or not, his career was flagging in his fifties, and I had the impression if this job didn't pan out, he had nowhere else to go. That night he was dressed all in black, like a riverboat gambler. His greying hair was covered by a silver turban with an enormous fake ruby in the middle—all the better to cement his celebrity status with the clientele.

And that, ladies and gents, was the cast of characters for the evening.

The menu was simple but elegant—puree of squash, Cajun-blackened salmon, rice pilaf, and grilled asparagus with hollandaise.

Cat and I were confident and sure-handed, balancing the serving trays as smoothly as The Mansion's resident juggler—that was until Billy Whitlock, whose baby brown eyes had been glued to Cat's swaying backside all night, suddenly whipped sideways to stare at her as she bent over to retrieve a dropped napkin from the floor. The bowl of soup I was about to set in front of him tipped backward when he hit it and landed on my chest before falling to the floor. The lovely puree, of course, stayed on the front of my service uniform.

All eyes turned to me as I scrambled to pick up the bowl off the floor. "Sorry," I said.

"No, dude, it's all me," Billy said, his Adam's apple bobbing up and down in this throat. I swore he looked at me like he wanted to lick it all off, but I didn't say anything else. Seriously? Hadn't he ever seen a woman bend over before?

While I stood back and took a napkin to my soup-laden chest, Cecile Elway lifted her hand to Fabrizio. "Oh, Fabrizio," she cooed, "I forgot to mention we have a special requirement for the séance." She exchanged a meaningful look with her psychic, who nodded what I interpreted to be encouragement. Cecile went on, "And since it's just the tiniest bit unusual, I wanted you to have ample notice for its procurement."

Fabrizio, with lifted chin and half-closed eyes in full-on medium character, smiled and said, "Of course, madam—"

As I turned to go back to the kitchen and change into a clean uniform, Mrs. Elway gushed, "Oh, Cecile, please," and batted her lashes, flirting with Fabrizio like a schoolgirl. She crooked a finger at him and whispered in his ear as he leaned his head toward her.

When she finished, he pulled away and gave her a look I can only describe as dumbfounded. "Really?" he asked. "For the séance?"

She smiled and nodded.

"Did I hear you correctly?" He stammered a little. "Did you say...clams?"

CHAPTER TWO

———

By the time we finished with the dinner service, the ferry had quit running, so Cat and I couldn't make it home. Jack found an empty room for us. It was on the second floor in the auxiliary wing about as far away from the main building as you could get, and the remodel hadn't reached it yet, but the beds were soft, the linens dense and luxurious. We both slept like newborns in the T-shirts we wore to work. The next morning we dressed for work in a fresh change of costumes housekeeping had put in our lockers.

Cat had an early appointment. My first, the elaborate Gryffindor crest, wasn't until ten thirty. I was in the employee lounge lingering over a cup of chicory (so strong it threatened to straighten my hair) and a warm cream cheese pastry (so yummy I was pretty sure it had been concocted by a voodoo priestess).

"Melanie, my girl, just like your name, your song strums the strings of my heart."

"Good morning, Fabrizio."

Some of the performers at the hotel worked the day shift—Cat, me, the masseuse, Mambo the voodoo priestess, for example. The entertainers took the evening shift—the magicians and Aurelia the Aura Reader fell into that category, the musicians, of course, and so did Fabrizio.

Fabrizio lived on the island in *la petite maison* with his sweetie, Harry Villars. He was seldom seen at The Mansion itself unless he was working.

I turned. "What are you doing here so early?"

He was dressed like a regular Joe that morning in a golf shirt and a pair of faded jeans. No eyeliner or pancake makeup. I liked him better that way. He sat down across from me and drew circles on the table with his index finger until the buff twentysomething golden boy who gave massages refilled his cup and left the room, and I was alone with Fabrizio.

"I've a favor to ask, m'dear," he began.

I smiled at him over my cup. "You know I can't refuse you."

He patted my hand. My grandparents took care of me when I was a child. They were aging flower children and encouraged me to express myself in whatever way I wished. My grandfather owned a detail shop where he painted cars and motorcycles with flames, buxom women, and skulls. It was where I learned about design. He died when I was eighteen, and I still missed him every day.

Fabrizio looked just like him, right down to the longish, grey locks he sometimes slicked back and put in a ponytail.

Being a gay man and only recently liberated, Fabrizio was never blessed with offspring. He and I had sort of adopted each other.

"The séance Mrs. Elway booked to contact her deceased husband, Theodore Elway, is set for seven thirty this evening."

I nodded. We had all been told why Cecile Elway and her family had come.

He went on. "I was hoping you'd consent to staying over tonight to sit in on it."

Hmm. "Well…why?"

"Mr. Stockton…"

My heartbeat quickened. Really? Did I have it so bad that just the mention of Cap'n Jack's name got me going?

"…has declared there's a good deal riding on my performance tonight. He's indicated that Mrs. Elway and her psychic adviser, Ms. Devere, are in a position to bring a goodly amount of business to this fine establishment—that is, if all goes as they expect. And I worry for Harry's investment, as I'm sure you're well aware." His eyes went soft when he said Harry's name. The two had only been a couple a short while but seemed totally devoted to each other. "Not only that, but Mrs. Elway has promised me personally a bonus of a hundred thousand dollars if I'm successful in…" he paused, "…contacting the late Mr. Elway."

Everyone who worked at The Mansion knew all the supernaturalists hired by Harry Villars were just actors.

A hundred grand? Wow. "Well, that's a good thing. Isn't it? But," I asked, "what does that have to do with me?"

He pulled back his shoulders and raised his chin. So dramatic. "I've prepared for tonight as much as I possibly can. It will be one of the premier performances of my career. While stage fright has never been a malady with which I'm afflicted, I would be uttering an untruth if I denied that I'm bloody well scared to death."

He lifted his eyes to mine, eyes just like Gramps's—eyes I knew I couldn't deny.

"I need your moral support, my dear. It's that simple."

I reached across the table and covered our two hands with my other. "Of course," I said. "I'm yours for the evening, sir."

* * *

In the afternoon, I took the ferry back across to the Big Easy. If I had to spend yet another night at The Mansion, I wanted to have a change of clothes, my cell phone charger, and an assortment of all the other little things a girl needs to make it through the night. I packed a bag for Catalina as well. If I had to stay over, I wanted sympathetic company.

As the ferry carried me back across to Mystic Isle, George slipped up beside me. "Y'at, Melanie?" he said. "You flying solo today? Where's your partner in crime—Miss Cat?"

The hope on his face was a beacon.

Cat was a good person, one of the best, and consciously never did anything to hurt anyone's feelings, so she'd never consider shunning George. She said it would "harvest bad karma."

But it made me sad that he wore his heart on his sleeve when he had absolutely no chance of winning her. "You know, George," I began, "Catalina has been seeing someone for quite a while now. They're very close. He's just gaga over her," *Like everyone else.* "And she's just as crazy about him." *Even though that cocky Cajun can be more pain in the patoot than he's worth sometimes.*

He smiled that big old Howdy Doody grin and bobbed his head. "Oh, yes, dawlin', I know. Deputy Quincy Boudreaux, he comes around all the time just to make sure I know Miss Catalina's well-being is real important to him, and I best be payin' all kinds of attention to my job while she's aboard."

"Oh," I said. "So you know about Quincy and Cat?"

"Aw, hell, Miss Melanie—pardon my language—ain't nobody in N'awlins don't know 'bout Deputy Quincy."

* * *

It was after six o'clock by the time I'd dressed in what I hoped was appropriate attire for a séance—long-sleeved, V-necked black dress. I put my hair up with an elaborate comb studded with fake emeralds I'd found at a secondhand store in the Quarter. The room phone rang, and I was summoned to the kitchen by Chef Valentine Cantrell.

Curious as hell, I went straight there.

The Mansion's kitchen had been added on around the turn of the century. Once there were no more slaves to haul the food from the original kitchen located in an outbuilding, the plantation owners added a regular kitchen on to the house. It had been updated through the decades, the most recent renovation only a couple of years earlier when The Mansion was converted to a hotel, and expanses of stainless steel surfaces and commercial appliances became the dominant elements.

The lovely Valentine Cantrell ruled over it like a Creole queen, a soup ladle her scepter, her crown the elasticized plastic cap over her Afro.

I walked in to find her chastising a kitchen worker for under seasoning the crawfish *etoufee* bubbling on the stove.

"Miss Melanie, my favorite skin-painting woman, yes?"

I curtsied. "At your service, Lady Cantrell."

She waved a hand at me. "You go on with yourself, now." Ladling stew into a clay bowl, she sprinkled cayenne on top and set it on a nearby stainless steel table beside a basket of fresh cornbread. "You eat now, girl. Can't be conversing with no spirits on an empty stomach."

I didn't hesitate but sat down and dug right in. Valentine's crawfish stew was legendary. "How'd you know about the séance?" I asked.

"Oh, Fabrizio, he come down here a while back and say he need you to take something with you when you go dere."

I looked up at her. "What?"

"Never you mind," she said. "All in good time."

I sopped up the stew with the crusty bread and watched her work. It had been a real coup for The Mansion when Valentine Cantrell signed on, and from what I knew, she could pretty much write her own ticket. At thirty-six, she was famous among culinary circles. Her golden eyes were always crinkled and plump cheeks always creased in a pleasant smile. Skin like butterscotch satin gave her the exotic appeal of a movie star. A kind and generous nature made her as beautiful inside as out.

And the food. Nothing else like it inside the sixty-four parishes. For some of the hotel employees, the food and a chance to sit down to leftovers was why they came here to work. A true *lagniappe*, as Valentine herself would say, a bonus.

Jack walked in just as I was finishing. I looked up at him. The bright kitchen lights bounced off his dark hair, bringing out auburn highlights I'd never noticed before.

"Miss Hamilton," he said softly. How the heck did my name turn into an aphrodisiac coming from his lips? "You look amazing."

I'm embarrassed to tell you I batted my lashes. "Why thank you, Mr. Stockton."

"Did Chef Valentine talk to you about the clams?"

"Did you say…?" I looked over at Valentine, who was slaving over a chopping block, her knife reverberating like a machine gun. She didn't look up. She didn't dare if she wanted to keep all ten fingers.

"Clams," he repeated.

"Oh," I said. "No, she didn't get around to it yet."

He turned his head and lifted his chin, a New York gesture if I'd ever seen one, toward a stainless-steel kitchen cart against the wall. A clear glass dome covered a good-sized platter. Clams on the half shell sat atop a generous bed of salt crystals on the platter. Parsley and lemons decorated it.

"Clams?" I said again. "For the séance? I don't—"

"I didn't either at first," he interrupted. "But Fabrizio insisted Mrs. Elway asked for them specifically. A dozen fresh clams on the half shell. It seems they were her husband's favorite dish, and she is convinced having them there will encourage his—I can't believe I'm saying this—his spirit to manifest."

"Oh." What else was there to say? I glanced at my watch. "Well, looks like it's getting to be about that time." I stood.

He didn't step back from the table, which put me right next to him. I could have leaned over and laid my head on his shoulder. I sighed. *Better not.*

But Cap'n Jack seemed to have something similar on his mind. He laid his hand on my shoulder and leaned over me. I closed my eyes and held my breath, anticipating…what?

A soft cloth caressed my upper lip. I opened my eyes.

He smiled down at me. "There you go," he said and laid the napkin down. "You just had a little sauce there."

Of course I did. "Thank you," I said. "I'll just…"

I crossed the room, took hold of the cart's handle, and pushed it from the kitchen.

*   *   *

Séances were held in a small but lovely room where Miss Marple might serve tea. Burgundy drapes swagged corner to corner. Blue flames flickered low in the fireplace courtesy of a special-effects chemical log Fabrizio swore would bring up the ambiance.

A medium-sized round table sat smack in the middle of the room, seven chairs around it and a purple cloth covering it. The lights were low. So many candles were lit that the place was warm enough for bread to rise.

Fabrizio was already there, looking nervous as a crawfish next to a pot on the boil. He knew, and I knew, and he knew I knew he wasn't exactly what you'd call a genuine medium, but I had to give him credit. He looked like one, every inch, from the top of his turbaned head to the bottoms of his white patent-leather boots. His long face glistened with perspiration.

"Fabrizio," I said. "Why don't we blow out a few of these candles? Your makeup and eyeliner are going to run."

He nodded, and I set about doing it. The poor guy had to be pretty warm. His long-sleeved white jumpsuit was layered under a full-length sequined white cape. A cross between the Great Houdini and Liberace.

Within a few minutes, Mrs. Cecile Elway and company arrived. Five in all, just like at dinner the night before. There were low murmurs of appreciation as they glanced around the room, taking in the whole experience.

Fabrizio opened his arms wide. His bellowing voice carried all the drama of his training at the Royal Academy. "Welcome—welcome, all."

The group circled the room, all heads swiveling this way, that way, taking in the authentic ambiance the hotel owner's checkbook—fortified by a winning streak Harry and his cousins enjoyed on *Family Feud*—had bought.

Fabrizio lifted fingertips to his temples and closed his eyes. "Come, my friends, let us be seated. I sense the spirits gathering."

Glancing around nervously, they all converged on the table where Fabrizio stood in front of a high-backed chair with a red velvet seat that looked more like a throne than anything else.

"Hey, I remember you." Billy Whitlock, Cecile's stepgrandson, peered at me in the semidarkness. "You're the girl from last night. Right?" His eyes dipped below my chin to my cleavage. "I see you're not wearing the soup tonight."

Well, wasn't that special? *Nice to be remembered.* I tried to smile.

Cecile seemed to have just noticed me. "Who is that young woman, and what is she doing here? This is supposed to be an exclusive affair."

Mrs. Elway looked doubtful until Fabrizio took her hand and patted it. "Miss Hamilton is here at my invitation. She's been known to be a soul sympathetic to the world beyond the veil, an asset when summoning spirits. Mrs. Elway, if you would sit to my right, please. Miss Hamilton to my left." He glanced around to the others and spread his arms to indicate the empty chairs.

Cecile took the chair to Fabrizio's right. Terrence Montague, who I'd decided was shacking up with Mrs. Elway on behalf of his caterpillar conservancy organization, took the chair next to Cecile.

Rosalyn, the stepdaughter, twittered like a nervous little bird as she sat down beside him.

Penny Devere, the psychic, was opposite Fabrizio. Billy Whitlock flipped the next chair backward and straddled it. The remaining chair looked like it had my name on it.

The look on Billy's young face said a lot about his attitude, and his words only served to confirm it. "Really? This is uberlame."

"Billy, shush." His mother put a finger to her thin lips.

Fabrizio clasped a hand to his forehead, his expression pained. "We must all be of like mind as we call on your grandfather's spirit. We must have harmony, or the psychic energy will not flow freely."

"Harmony? What a crock."

"That will be enough, Billy!" Mrs. Elway said.

When it came to séances, I pretty much agreed with Billy.

Everyone settled in.

"As you glance around the room," Fabrizio began, "you'll be aware of the tools required to summon your loved one." He rolled his hands over his "crystal ball." I was pretty sure it was a big snow globe he appropriated from the reading room. "A bell for Theodore to signal us when he's arrived." Fabrizio's eyes cut over to me then back to Cecile. "Did you bring a picture of Theodore with you as I asked?"

Cecile fished in her big purse and pulled out a small photo, which she handed to Fabrizio.

He laid it on the table beside the crystal ball. "Everyone must join hands, close your eyes," he said, "and open your minds."

As silence settled over the room, Penny Devere looked around the table. "Do we have everything we need?"

Cecile spoke suddenly. "Oh," she said, "the clams. Don't forget the..."

I disengaged from the minor tussle with young Billy, who'd been trying to stroke my palm when our hands were clasped, and stood, went to the trolley, took the cover off the tray, and picked it up.

"Where should I...?"

Fabrizio glanced up then over at Cecile. "Put them in front of Mrs. Elway, please."

I carefully set them before her.

Rosalyn took a hanky from her bag and covered the lower half of her face.

Billy waved his hand in front of his face. "Ew, really? Gross."

Cecile only smiled. "Theodore's favorite. He always came to the table when we served clams on the half shell."

I actually didn't think they smelled bad. To each his own. I took my seat at the table as the Great Fabrizio went into his act.

He closed his eyes and threw back his head. His voice deepened. "Center yourselves. Reach out with your minds and souls. Think of your loved one. Call him."

The voices sounded.

"Theo?" Cecile's tone was uncertain.

Terrence Montague mumbled something I couldn't quite understand, but I could have sworn it sounded like, "Yeah, whatever."

"Daddy," Rosalyn twittered. "Daddy?"

"Mr. Elway." That was Penny, her voice soft. "Theodore."

"Hey, Granddad. S'up?" Billy's voice rang above everyone else's.

Fabrizio cleared his throat. "I feel the vibrations. Theodore? Theodore? Our beloved Theodore, we bring you gifts from life into death. Commune with us, Theodore, and move among us. Give us a sign."

The room grew cold as a stiff breeze circled the room, extinguishing the candles. The lights went out. I couldn't have seen my hand in front of my face. A collective gasp circled the table.

The bell tinkled, fell over, and rolled across the table.

It was Fabrizio speaking, but it wasn't his voice or accent. "Dammit all, Cecile, you forgot the hot sauce."

Cecile cried out. "Oh. Oh. Theo? Theo, I'm sorry. I'm so sorry."

"Simple questions, Mrs. Elway," Fabrizio said, his normal pitch and British accent back. "Only yes or no questions."

"Daddy! Daddy!" It was Rosalyn's voice. "Daddy, tell us. How did you really die? Did someone murder you?"

A soft moaning came from somewhere above us. The table began to vibrate then to shake. And then the crazy thing lifted off the floor.

"Whoa, dude." Billy seemed to be enjoying the show.

If I hadn't known better myself, I'd have believed old Theodore had joined us. The table crashed back down. And suddenly I wasn't holding anyone's hand anymore. There were soft whimpers, the scraping sound of chairs scooting back, and feet shuffling.

It was scary. *Damn, Fabrizio. Good job.*

The room grew quiet. No one seemed to be moving anymore.

The only sound in the room was the low hum of Fabrizio's voice as he continued with the farce, staying fully "connected" to the spirit world. After a few minutes, the lights came back on for no apparent reason I could see.

Everyone had stood and moved away from the table except Fabrizio, who was still in his chair, eyes closed. The rest of us all looked around the room at each other, relieved to have made it all the way back from the world beyond.

Or maybe we all hadn't made it after all.

Cecile Elway was still in her chair, slumped over, her face buried in the platter of clams. A few empty clamshells were strewn around in front of her.

Montague lifted her wrist and let it drop back. "My word," he said. "I believe she's...but she can't be. Can she?" He looked around at all of us. "Dead? She can't be dead."

But she was.

"Hmm," Billy said. "Bad clams?"

CHAPTER THREE

———

Deputy Quincy Boudreaux of Jefferson Parish Sheriff's Office was a dream of a man with big brown eyes and brown-tipped blond hair. Cute enough all right, but there was a slight problem with Quincy. There was helter-skelter in those beautiful peepers, and his hair always stuck up all over like he just got out of bed, which combined to give him the look of a recent escapee from the state wacky shack over in Jackson. If the man didn't wear a badge on his chest and a gun on his hip, you'd think twice about being around him. You might think twice about being around him anyway.

Quincy Boudreaux was Cajun, born and bred in the bayou, and he was stone-cold crazy about my beautiful bestie. And she about him. It was a tempestuous love affair worthy of a Margaret Mitchell novel. I'd never felt that fire before. All my relationships to date had been sweet and calm, more platonic than anything else. I'd be lying if I said the passion Cat and Quincy stirred up didn't make me a little envious. That is, until Cap'n Jack showed up. Whenever that man came around, it was like someone struck a match in my pants. I had high hopes of someday being able to do something about that.

Deputy Quincy and a couple of other nice boys from Jefferson Parish Sheriff's Office showed up at The Mansion about a half hour after we let the department know about Cecile Elway.

Those of us who'd been in the séance room all stood on the veranda while they wheeled poor Mrs. Elway, all zipped up in a plastic body bag, out through the front entrance. The welcome dirge played appropriately every time someone walked in or out.

"Will somebody please turn that off?" Quincy said a bit too loud.

Jack walked up just as they loaded the gurney into the ambulance. "Make it happen," he called back over his shoulder to the reception desk, and the dreary organ music stopped abruptly. Jack stood beside me.

"Just exactly what's he doing?" Jack squinted into the night.

Lurch leaned up against the rear door of the ambulance where the paramedics wrestled the gurney with poor Mrs. Elway into the ambulance.

"Oh," I said when I saw what was going on.

"Ohmigod," Jack burst out. "Lurch! Stop that right now."

Lurch looked up. He was as shamefaced as a third-grade boy caught sneaking into the girls' bathroom at school—but not ashamed enough to abstain from snapping off another selfie of him and the body bag.

Jack hung his head and sighed.

While he was looking for a suitable place to live in town, Mr. Villars had given Jack the use of the honeymoon cottage at the back of the property. Poor Cap'n Jack was always on site and consequently nearly always on the job.

He was dressed in jeans and a black T-shirt. I'd never seen him in anything but a suit, and I couldn't take my eyes off his strong arms and the planes of his hard chest and abs outlined against the tight cotton knit. His dark hair was ruffled like he'd been running his hands through it. He was close enough I caught his scent. I once had asked him what it was, and he'd shrugged and smiled and said, "Bleu. Chanel," then with a shy smile, "you like it?"

I did like it. It was fresh, yet sensual, and allowed a secondary unique scent to come through, what I called Eau de Cap'n Jack, clean, manly.

He put his arm around my shoulder and looked down at me in concern. "How are you doing, Miss Hamilton?" His voice was low. "I'm so sorry you had to experience that."

Oh, my. I couldn't help myself. I had a little trouble breathing. If it were a hundred and fifty years ago, I'd have said I had a bad case of the vapors. Translated to the twenty-first century for y'all, I was turned on.

The blip then rising yelp of the siren snapped me out of it, and I was instantly ashamed. Poor Mrs. Elway.

Quincy sucked his teeth and shook his head. "Nothing like bagging up a good stiff to start an eight-hour shift. Let's get dis done." He turned and went to the door.

Jack, Cat, and I stood outside under the portico in the still of the bayou night. Wispy clouds moved across the moon, playing hide and seek over the cypress trees. Crickets and frogs serenaded each other. The occasional splash foretold the entry of a gator moving in the water, maybe chasing dinner. It was a beautiful night if you didn't count somebody dying right in front of me.

Lurch was enormous, over seven feet tall, and his shoulders had to be half again that broad. He always turned sideways and ducked to get through most doors in the hotel, but he could carry enough bags to check in half a dozen guests in one trip. We nicknamed him Lurch, and everyone called him that. I don't think anyone but the HR Department knew his real name. Now, having been denied further selfie activity, he stood just inside the lobby, shaking his big old head and moaning at the grim goings-on in front of The Mansion.

The ambulance disappeared behind a grove of cypress around the bend in the road.

"Y'all coming?" Quincy led us all back through the hotel lobby where the rest of the looky-lou hotel guests and staff members stood around craning their necks and whispering to each other. We followed tiredly to the rear of the main building and the séance room.

Jack, Cat, and I waited in the open doorway. I was kind of creeped out after what happened there, but the lights were all on now, and aside from all the crime scene tape and evidence markers, the place looked pretty normal. A couple of deputies went around the room photographing everything. One of them came over and unapologetically took several shots of Cat, the rapid-fire shutter on his camera clicking like castanets. She posed dramatically. Quincy chased him off.

A stout middle-aged woman I'd never seen before stood at the table, dropping the slimy clamshells one at a time into a clear plastic bag. "Who's that?" I asked.

"My friend from the parish medical center. She helps us out since Jefferson Parish be too small for an official coroner," Quincy explained. "She be taking dem clams with her, y'all. We don't like da look of 'em."

Quincy jerked his head at us. "Let's leave 'em to it," he said. "Lead me to the kitchen."

Cat took hold of my hand as we walked, squeezing it. I squeezed back. She wasn't at the scene of the crime, didn't have to hang around for all this, but she did, and I knew it was for me. That was Cat.

The four of us made our way from the séance room in the farthest corner on the ground floor, back through the circular foyer where the grand staircase sat silently waiting for more glory days of Scarlett O'Hara descending with her hoopskirts and ringlets.

Cecile's family, Terrence, and Fabrizio had all been relocated to the main salon at the front of the house to give statements. We bypassed it and went behind the staircase to the lower level passageway to the kitchen.

Valentine sat at one of the tables drinking coffee. When we all walked in, she got up and brought the pot to the table along with four empty cups.

"Boy," Valentine said. Only Valentine Cantrell could get away with calling Deputy Quincy Boudreaux boy. "You better have one good reason f'true for making me come all the way back here tonight." Valentine lived over in Estelle in a pretty little red brick house with white trim and gardenia bushes in the front yard. I always figured that place she owned in Estelle, and the school and neighborhood where her eight-year-old son had put down roots were the reasons Harry Villars had been able to lure her to Mystic Isle. "What's up with all dem police cars?" she demanded.

Cat and I sat at the table. Jack sat beside me. Valentine poured us coffee—the strong scent of the steaming coffee and chicory was a dose of pure revival. I must have been looking a bit tired or something, because Jack patted my hand and gave me one of those sympathetic looks. I resisted the urge to put my arms around his neck and sit on his lap like Papa Noel. *Here's my Christmas list, Papa Noel. All I want you to bring me downriver in your bateaux is you in a Santa hat and thong.*

Quincy got out his phone and sent a text. Within a minute or two, a couple of deputies came to the kitchen.

"Now, Miss Valentine, we'll be needing the rest of those clams from the same batch you sent to the séance tonight."

She drew in an agitated breath. "Clams—"

"In fact," he went on. "We'll be needing whatever clams you have here altogether."

She didn't like it much. I could tell by the way her eyes spit daggers at him and the way she stood and smacked her palm down on the table. "You think I served them bad clams? Me? You think I don't be knowing the difference between a good clam and a bad one?"

He just smiled and spread his hands. "Now, Miss Valentine, don't take it personal. Y'all know I gotta cover all avenues, *chère*."

She stomped over to the big walk-in fridge at the far side of the room, went in, and came right back out with two enormous Ziploc bags full of clams still in the whole shell. From the hard squint of her eyes and the momentum of her carriage, I could have sworn she was going to throw them at him, but instead she plopped them down onto the counter then stood back, her hands on her hips. "Dere ya go, boy. I hope you're happy. These is the ones I was planning to use for my mama's special chowder. Now because of this silly boy and his suspicious mind, I ain't got nothing to fix for tomorrow's lunch menu."

She cast an exasperated look at Jack, who threw up his hands and shook his gorgeous head, obviously at a loss, like Valentine.

The two deputies came forward and loaded up a good-sized evidence bag with the clams then put them in a Styrofoam cooler and walked out.

Quincy cleared his throat and began to pace, hands behind his back. His brow was furrowed. He turned to Valentine, apology written all over his face. "Miss Valentine, darlin', I know you wouldn't serve no bad clams, but we have to check 'em all, or we won't be able to say whether there might have been something wrong with the ones she ate."

I couldn't help it. "You think it was the clams that killed her, Quincy?"

He shrugged. "Well, she dead, ain't she?"

"But you don't think Valentine had anything to do with it…?"

He smiled. "Course not. Look at dat woman—why, she a pillar of virtue, that one."

Valentine gave him a look, and then her face broke into a smile that beamed all the way to the state line. "Aw, boy." She waved her hand at him. "You try that sugar on someone who might be fool enough to lap it up."

He cocked his head and grinned. "And besides, Chef Cantrell, what motive could you possibly have to number one, serve bad clams, or number two, to kill off Miz Elway? I mean, you never even met her. Ain't dat right?"

He watched as Valentine smiled, sat back down at the table, and lifted her coffee mug.

"So, Chef," he went on, "who came to you asking for dem clams in the first place?"

Valentine's mouth drew into a hard line, and she shook her head.

Law of the bayou, I guessed. Don't ever rat anybody out. I knew who sent for the clams. Anyone who'd been in the dining room Saturday night knew who sent for the clams. Cecile Elway originated the request, but it would have been Fabrizio who went to Valentine to make sure they were available the next night for the séance.

"Come on now, Miss Valentine," Quincy cajoled. "You know you goin' tell me. Just get it done."

She shook her head. I'd never seen her look so grim.

Quincy leaned forward. "It was him, yes? The Great Fabrizio? He come to you asking for clams on the half shell. Right?"

She didn't move, not even a tick.

"You tell me now. It was him?"

Valentine looked at him a long minute, her tawny eyes sad. She drew in a breath and held it. The movement of her head was barely perceptible. By the look on her face, I knew she hated being put on the spot, but still, she nodded. "Fabrizio, yes. But he weren't the only one interested in dem clams."

Quincy leaned in and waited as she continued. "That other woman, the one who look like she need a man to relax her some?"

I hid a smile behind my hand. "Would that be Rosalyn Whitlock, Cecile's stepdaughter?"

"Yeah, dat one. Whitlock. She was down here before the séance asking 'bout the clams. Say she wanted to make sure everything was all set so she could talk to her daddy."

Quincy's eyes lit up. It was as if Valentine had given him a gift. "So," he spoke slowly. "The daughter, she was in here beforehand? And I ain't supposin' she was anywhere near dem clams, now was she?"

Valentine thought about it then. "Well, now you speak of it..."

All the intensity went out of Quincy. He patted her hand and sat back.

I had to give it to him. The Quincy Boudreaux I knew was always like a young pup just panting along after Catalina. I never had seen him on the job before. He was sly, that boy, and slick as honey on a warm biscuit.

With only a couple of questions, he'd pretty much already eliminated a murder suspect—but then, none of us ever really considered Valentine Cantrell, master chef and role model to every other chef south of Nashville, would be the one to either serve bad clams or taint them with something so vile as poison.

* * *

While Cat and Jack waited in the game room, Quincy and I went back to the main salon, where they wrapped up preliminary questioning of the six of us who were in the séance room at the time Cecile Elway died.

No one in the family knew of a history of heart disease. In fact, no one seemed to know anything except for the stepdaughter, Rosalyn Elway Whitlock, who was bound and determined it was the ghost of her father, Theodore Elway, who came back from the gates of hell and struck down his wife. "It was Daddy. I know it. I felt his presence." Her voice reminded me of an out-of-tune concertina.

She cast a meaningful look at Penny Devere, Mrs. Elway's resident psychic, who sat with her at one of the café tables where wine and cocktails were served during happy hour. Penny nodded gravely at Rosalyn's declaration, and Rosalyn took one of Penny's plump hands into her own.

Penny only said, "I've heard of it happening before. The hand of death can reach across the void."

I was on one of the antebellum-style love seats beside Fabrizio. We looked at each other and both rolled our eyes. I leaned over and whispered, "Please tell me you're not suddenly a legitimate medium…"

He gave a nearly imperceptible shake of his head.

"…who can summon expired heirs to the Pennsylvania steel industry, who then kill their wives before they bug out to the great beyond again."

Fabrizio turned his mouth to my ear and whispered back. "No, my dear, I'm no more a legitimate medium than you, unless you've been holding out on me."

I couldn't help it. Inappropriate as it was, I giggled.

Quincy shot me a look, and I swear I felt like I was back in second grade caught with a mouthful of bubble gum.

"Well," Quincy said, "I see we're all getting pretty tired tonight. So I'm going to let you go to your rooms. But I'm going to insist you remain here at The Mansion until I get my head around this case real good and proper, because right now I got an itch that we'll be learning Miz Elway didn't succumb to natural causes, and that someone, maybe even one of you, had a hand in sending her to that big *fais-do-do* in da sky."

Everyone, including me, let out a big sigh.

"Big what?" Billy's annoying voice was the first to break the silence in the room.

"*Fais-do-do*," Quincy said, smiling. "It's a big ol' party, and I just know we're all hoping your gran'mama up dere is having a high old time."

* * *

Cat and I headed back to our same room. Another night in the Louisiana swamp. I called our neighbor Monsieur Beauregard Taylor at Thibadeaux's Bar in the French Quarter, where he tended bar five nights a week.

When he answered, I said, "Beauregard, I have to stay over at The Mansion another night. Will you feed Satchmo and take a couple of minutes to rub his ears?"

"You know I will, *chère*," he said.

His low, sexy voice carried me back about a year ago when he and I had dated—if that was what you could call it. My definition of "dating" didn't quite match his, the objective of which seemed to be bringing home as many prospects as possible. I prefer my relationships one-on-one—you know, one gal and one guy. Beauregard was a big and beautiful Creole man who could put a woman flat on her back with just one look—not that those dreamy, seductive gazes worked with me. I grew up in this town surrounded by slow-talking men with smooth ways and that velvet Southern drawl, and they didn't affect me the way they did Yankee girls. Maybe that was part of the problem. Maybe my immunity to his enticing ways was the reason we just never really got anything going. I hadn't been interested in anyone since Beau, and I never really had much time for dating in college either. Those boys weren't interested in learning anything about me except what color my undies were anyway. I guess you could say the right man just hadn't moseyed my way yet.

Cat came out of the steamy bathroom in her nightshirt and plopped down on one of the beds. With her hair wet and her face scrubbed clean, she was the all-American girl next door every all-American boy next door dreamed about.

"You get hold of Beauregard?" she asked.

"I did." I picked up my makeup kit, a clean pair of undies, and my nightshirt and headed for the shower myself. "He'll have old Satchmo purring like crazy. By the time we make it back home, that cat will think we're newcomers to the neighborhood."

The shower was divine. I really needed it. I hadn't even known Cecile Elway, but I couldn't stop wondering about her, about all the things she'd never get to do, all the Christmases and birthdays she was going to miss. I felt pretty bad about the whole darn thing.

Cat was propped up on two pillows, messing with her cell phone when I returned to the room, threw back the covers, and crawled into bed.

"What do you think?" I asked her.

"About what happened?"

"Yeah, that. I mean, I can't believe any of those people would be able to actually—you know—murder Mrs. Elway."

Cat looked across at me from her bed and shrugged. "I dunno," she said, "but it doesn't seem likely. You were there— what do you think?"

I switched off the bedside lamp.

It was quiet in the room. The clock on the nightstand ticked so loudly you would have thought it'd be detonating any second. The bathroom pipes shuddered. The sounds of the bayou seeped in through the window—the guttural croaking of a hundred frogs, the grating chirp of crickets scissoring their legs together. A nearby owl hooted mournfully—if he were warning us of imminent death, as was widely believed in the bayou, the fool was too late.

"I dunno either."

Across the room, an old portrait of grim Alphonse Villars was lit by a direct beam of moonlight from the window on the opposite wall.

It wasn't a flattering portrait of Harry's great-great-grandfather to begin with, and the way the moon shone on it was fairly spooky.

"Cat?"

"Mmm?" She sounded drowsy.

"You believe in ghosts?"

She didn't answer right away then, "I do."

"Do you believe like Penny Devere said, they can reach across the void and do harm?"

Again, she said, "I do."

"Do you think maybe Cecile's stepdaughter Rosalyn might be right? Maybe the ghost of Theodore Elway did her in?"

"Nah," we said in unison.

"No way." I tried to laugh, but it was forced.

I lay still in the darkness, staring at the disturbing painting of the old man and wondering if there was indeed a world unseen where those who'd left this one dwelt, planning their revenge against those of us they perceived had done them ill. I shuddered at the thought. Grandmama Ida believed in those things. And while my mama went to all kinds of trouble to discourage her, my grandmama still went about the business of keeping bad things away from her and those she loved.

Her house, where I spent most of my childhood days while my mother managed Ruby's Famous Bourbon Chicken in the Holy Cross neighborhood, was loaded with candles, amulets, sacks of herbs, and other talismans to ward off evil—even haint blue paint to keep enthusiastic haints out of the place. I took these things in stride. And although I knew all about them, I wasn't particularly superstitious and never put much store in tales of things that go bump in the night.

But tonight? Well, that was something else.

I turned my head slightly, and I swore I saw Alphonse's eyes turn with it. No way. I blinked hard then looked again, lifting my chin to stare down my nose. Even that angle supported the fact the old fart in the portrait was watching me.

"Cat? That picture's got me spooked."

"Spooked?" She rose up on one elbow and fixed her eyes on it. "Don't look at it." She plumped her pillow, pulled the sheet up, and rolled over.

"I can't help it. I think it's watching me." I pulled one of my pillows out from under my head and covered my face with it, but just like a six-year-old, I lifted one corner to peek out.

Yep. Still staring. I sighed, got up, took my robe off the foot of the bed, and hung it over the painting.

Better. Much better. I lay back down and went straight to sleep.

CHAPTER FOUR

———

Mardi Gras colors—purple, green, and gold. A delicate fairy with dragonfly wings and a dress made of ivy leaves had fully materialized on my client's right shoulder about the time Deputy Quincy sashayed into the parlor.

"Hoo-wee." He whistled, leaning over for a look at the tattoo. "Would you look at dat?"

I finished up and wiped the work down with alcohol then handed my customer a mirror to check out the finished work.

She paid me, left a really nice tip, threw on a jacket over her tube top, and left.

"We got the word on them clams," Quincy said. "Just like I thought. They was poisoned. That poor old gal, she never had no chance."

I spread my hands out in front of me. "You don't think I had anything to do with it, do you?"

He shook his head. "No, *chère*. Not you."

I kept my eyes on him while slipping off my latex gloves. "Poisoned? F'sure?" It was terrible news for the hotel, for Jack—someone being murdered during a séance, one of the most often booked services at The Mansion, and on Jack's watch.

"My friend up at the lab, she still working on it. Going to be telling me what kind of poison real soon now, but in the meantime, *chère*, you hear anything, you let me know." He turned to leave, but stopped. "You seen Cat?"

"She's working. Said she had a full day."

He nodded. "You catch up to her, you maybe please tell her I'm free for lunch. I hear Valentine's whipped up some shrimp po'boys." He shook his gorgeous head. "She cooks like an angel, dat woman."

He walked off whistling. I surely liked Quincy. He made me smile. I figured that was one of the things Cat liked about him too.

After Quincy left, it was as if my parlor had a revolving door. First Cat came around to tell me that Quincy stopped by to see her and that she was joining him for lunch, and then almost word for word, she repeated what Quincy said about the clams.

Next it was Jack's turn. He brought me a regular coffee, and we sat down together while he told me that Quincy stopped by to see him too. Then again, almost word for word, he repeated what Quincy said about the clams poisoning Cecile Elway.

I listened politely, and by the time he was done speaking, between him and Cat, I knew backward and forward every word that came out of Quincy Boudreaux's mouth, in addition to those I'd heard from Q. After a while Jack began to talk about his job.

"Terrible thing, this death. The deputy thinks it's homicide." He paused. "Not that it's about me at all, but I'm nervous how this will look to my employer. It can't bode well for my job security."

"This is the deep South, Jack," I said. "Folks down here aren't quick to jump to conclusions, and I can't believe anyone would think this was your fault anyway."

He shrugged then. "Maybe. Maybe not. Either way, I need to watch my p's and q's, and part of that has to do with you."

"Me?"

He nodded. "As much as I'd like to see you away from work, get to know you better..."

My heart started to pound so hard, I was pretty sure he could hear it.

"...I don't dare. I'm your boss. Our seeing each other could lead to all sorts of issues."

Oh. Was this his way of letting me down easy? Or was this his way of saying he was hot for me?

I was confused.

Jack got up and walked over to where I kept my portfolio of designs to inspire tattoo customers.

He absent-mindedly thumbed through it. "You know you're really good, Mel. You ever do any real painting?"

He didn't look up when he spoke, and I had the feeling my designs weren't really what he had on his mind.

"Yes," I said. "I do. I paint N'awlins street scenes and the like. People seem to appreciate my stuff. Sometimes I sell one or two."

He did look up then. "Really? Good for you. Maybe someday you'll leave this place and make a name for yourself as an artist."

"Well now, for the time being, I'm just glad for the chance to make a little extra for the cause."

He came back and sat down again. "I heard you're part of a movement restoring some of the hardest hit neighborhoods destroyed by Katrina."

"Yes," I said softly and took the opportunity to inspect the backs of my hands. I don't like talking much about that. Makes me look like I think I'm a saint or something. Saintly, I'm not.

"That's generous of you," he said. "You seem like a really, really good person to me."

"Nah, you go on. I'm just like anyone in N'awlins who sees a job needs doing and rolls up her sleeves."

"There're people like that in New York too. We saw a lot of them after 9/11," he said. "Good people. Men and women."

Women. I took a deep breath. "Good-looker like you, I bet you knew a lot of women up in the city."

"Maybe," he said. "Yes." He looked right at me, and my stomach clenched, but I couldn't look away. "But none like you, Mel. Not a single one like you."

* * *

My last appointment for the day left at two forty-five. Seeing as how I was stuck at The Mansion in spite of my personal preference, Jack okayed a swim in the gorgeous Olympic indoor pool at the resort, a remnant of the Gatsby glory days of the 1920s. Cerulean tiles with gold swirls were inlaid throughout. It was a masterpiece. The water reflected the blue and gold, and the effect was that of a magical lagoon.

I lifted my head on lap thirty and was startled by Fabrizio, standing on the edge.

"Hey." I stopped and looked up at him, treading water.

"Hello, my dear, excellent stroke."

He looked tired. His long face sagged with worry or fatigue or both. I didn't remember ever seeing him that way before.

I swam to the edge where he hunkered down, wobbling a little as he did so.

"What's up, Fabrizio?"

He shook his head. "There isn't much out there for an old thespian with bad knees."

Odd way to start a conversation. "Hmm," I said. "Guess it's a good thing you have this gig then."

He shook his head sadly and sighed as if the weight of the world rode on his bony shoulders. "Yes, I suppose. Lucky to have this," he paused and added a flourish to the word, "*gig* and lucky to have Harry. Especially to have Harry. I don't know what a genteel man like that sees in an old broken-down performer such as I. I never thought someone like Harry would want someone like me."

I reached out and touched his hand, being careful not to sling water all over him. "What is it, Fabrizio? I've never seen you like this."

He sighed. "I suppose I'm just a bit emotional, what with all that's happened. Feeling a little at loose ends, as they say. I so wanted to succeed with the Elway woman. It meant a great deal to me."

I didn't say it out loud, but it struck me that he'd taken this terrible thing that happened to Mrs. Elway and somehow made it about him.

"You know, my dear, that bonus money was earmarked for a good cause. A very good cause. I think I know you, in particular, have a weakness for good causes."

"Good cause?"

"Harry has a balloon payment coming up on the property remodel. I was going to give the money to him."

Harry and Fabrizio were the sweetest couple I knew. So caring, so considerate, not to mention generous. "Maybe you should speak to the stepdaughter. She might honor Cecile's promise. She even seemed more keen to hear from Mr. Elway than his wife."

He seemed to perk up a little at that and reached down to pat my wet head. "Brilliant, my dear." He beamed, seeming to feel better about things. "Absolutely brilliant. I'll seek her out this very minute." He stood. "You should continue with your laps."

"Nah, I'm done," I said. "I lost count."

He walked away, tossing back over his shoulder, "Thirty. I counted thirty."

* * *

An evening mist settled over the lake. Somewhere on the far bank a gator splashed into the water, looking for dinner. The cricket song was swinging into full chorus. My own was waiting for me in the kitchen where all us employees would gather in the staff dining room. On Mondays, Valentine prepared either sausage-and-okra gumbo or red beans and rice. For dessert, melt-in-your-mouth bread pudding with bourbon sauce. I was excited about a hot meal. It was a rare occasion I wound up at the resort at suppertime. Cat and Mel's place tended to serve items that came out of the freezer in a box or out of the pantry in a can. I was honestly hoping Chef went with the beans and rice tonight. It was a chore picking the okra from the gumbo—nasty stuff. I didn't care how healthy it was, I just plain old didn't like it.

I stood there a few minutes longer trying to figure out a way I could cozy up to Cap'n Jack without either of us getting in trouble with Harry Villars, the owner. An appropriate solution didn't pop into my head right away, and my stomach was starting to growl.

I turned from where I stood at the end of the wooden dock and started back for the main building and Valentine's hot dinner. An SUV from the Jefferson Parish Sheriff's Office sat in the circular driveway under the portico.

Quincy. He wouldn't be there if he didn't have something new. I started to jog. God forbid I should miss even the smallest bit of news.

Just as I approached the front, two deputies, one Quincy, one I didn't recognize, came out the double-wide doors with Fabrizio walking between them. His hands were cuffed behind him. The face he made when he saw me was tragic at the very least, suffering and full of shame at the very most.

What in blue blazes was going on?

Quincy stopped beside me as the other deputy moved toward the SUV with Fabrizio in tow.

"What's going on, Quincy?" I looked from Quincy to Fabrizio. "Fabrizio? Why are you—"

Quincy took hold of my arm and turned me to face him. "So sorry, *chère*. I know he a friend of yours."

"But what? Why?" I was dumbstruck.

"Dat Terrence fella say he's the victim's main squeeze, say the lady brought some big money down here to the swamps, say I should check it out."

"So...?"

"I did. No big money in the lady's room."

I didn't understand what that had to do with taking my friend away in cuffs. "So it wasn't in her room. Maybe she had them put it in the hotel safe."

He shrugged and looked truly unhappy about all this. "No, girl, not there either. But den I check out Fabrizio's room, and I was damn sad to find big money hiding there."

"What?" I couldn't believe it. Hadn't my friend just told me he wasn't going to get that hundred thousand she promised him? What changed? "Fabrizio had the money?"

Quincy shrugged. "Some of it anyway. Ten thousand in nice, crisp, bee-u-tiful hundred-dollar bills. Now, I ask you, how you think he come by that money?"

The last vestiges of dusk left the sky, and the mood lighting came on. Fabrizio didn't have ten thousand dollars to his name, much less in cash kept in his room. It didn't make any sense.

"You're taking him away because..."

"Because we thinking he take dat big money."

"You think he stole from Mrs. Elway?" I shook my head. If I didn't believe it, how could Quincy?

I turned my head away and noticed Jack standing to one side of the open doors. How long had he been there? Did he believe Fabrizio stole the money?

"Dat I do," Quincy said with a big sigh. "It's a right shame, it is. We just hoping he didn't kill her, too, while he at it."

CHAPTER FIVE

———

"Damn that Quincy!"

Cat got that hurt look on her face I knew so well. "Why would you say that? Poor thing, he just can't help it, Mel. He has to do those mean things. It's his job."

My hands seemed to have a mind of their own. They kept waving at her. "Cat! He took Fabrizio! To jail! *Our* Fabrizio!"

She put her arm around my shoulders and leaned her head against mine. I loved that about her. The resort might have hired her to read tarot cards, but in my opinion, she was more empath than anything else, always in tune to what others felt.

We had caught the ferry back across the river, and then because it was early enough that the streets were still busy with tourists, shoppers, and diners, we walked the few blocks to our place.

Cat and I split the outrageous rent in a two-bedroom apartment, an old two-story brick building facing Dumaine Street. You wouldn't ever think our apartment was cute just looking at the plain face, but it opened onto a beautiful little paved courtyard that said old New Orleans with a French accent—*ooh-la-la.*

The green shutters, wrought iron patio benches, and potted palms said, "*Bienvenue, mademoiselle.*"

Before we even put our bags down by the double French doors, our beautiful Satchmo, one of a very special litter of kittens whelped at The Mansion, came running from my bedroom and curled around my leg. I reached down to scratch him behind the ears.

Cat carried her bag into her bedroom. "Hot shower first then I'll take care of the dishes we left in the sink Saturday morning."

"Good." They were her dishes anyway. Cat ate breakfast at home while I'd gotten my sugar fix at Café du Monde that morning.

I snagged an apple out of the bowl on the counter and wandered back into the living room, where my half-finished painting of our lovely little courtyard sat alone and neglected on its easel, awaiting my further TLC. I had the feeling it would be a while before I could get back to it.

I took care of the litter box and gave Satchmo fresh food and water. Like any good neighbor, Beauregard was always kind enough to help us out with Satchmo when we drew overtime or took a weekender to the Gulf Coast casinos. Cat and I, in turn, helped him handle his laundry, which always seemed to be just a bit beyond him. He would have pink socks and underwear if left to his own devices. I often suspected he did it on purpose just so we'd feel sorry for him and give him a hand. Typical Southern man.

Thoughts about the terrible thing that happened at The Mansion and about poor Fabrizio sitting in a cell in the Jefferson Parish jail had been racing through my mind at Mach three. I heard the shower running, saw that the door wasn't closed all the way, and went into the bathroom. The curtain was drawn, and Cat was already splashing away, singing some Zydeco song Quincy had taught her.

I closed the lid then sat on the toilet. "Cat?"

She didn't stop singing.

I said it again, louder. "Cat?"

She grabbed the edge of the curtain and poked her head out. "Hey," she said. "What?"

It took nearly fifteen minutes to convince her Fabrizio needed our help in beating this bad rap and that we needed to go back to Mystic Isle, dig around, and see if we could find anything. I truly believe the only reason she finally agreed was that she was turning into a prune.

We took Satchmo and his traveling gear over to Beauregard next door.

He pulled a late shift and was just getting ready to go to work. Beauregard was one of the most colorful bartenders on Bourbon Street. His finesse with a bottle and a shaker was legendary.

He agreed to watch Satchmo for as long as we needed, which left us girls free to undertake our recon mission.

* * *

It was pouring rain as George took us back across on the ferry, so Cat and I sat together in the middle under the canopy. The rain let up and stopped within minutes of docking on the opposite bank. Cat talked George into letting us use his car, parked in the employee lot at the ferry dock, to drive to the resort.

His car turned out to be a shabby army-green Volvo station wagon, circa 1975 or so. In the hazy glow of pole lights, the thing looked like a big old toad squatting in the middle of the parking lot.

He handed the key to Cat like it was a frickin' Bentley, for crying out loud. "Your carriage, Princess Catalina."

Sheese.

Inside, the car was every bit as wrecked as one would expect from a vehicle of that ancient age. The seats were worn so thin in spots the foam stuck up. A blanket was draped over the backseat. Cat and I looked at each other. It wasn't necessary to say neither of us was interested in what lay beneath that dusty old thing.

So as not to seem like we didn't appreciate the use of the vehicle, we both hugged George before getting in, starting it up—sort of—and driving away. The poor old thing coughed and choked like a three-pack-a-day smoker. But we were up and mobile and making our way along the unlit bayou back road that wound its way to Mystic Isle.

At least we were for a while.

After about twenty minutes, or maybe three-quarters of the way there, the ancient Swede burped, wheezed, and stopped dead.

Cat tried her best to get the engine to do something, but even her most persuasive sweet talk and gentle stroking were to no avail. The car was dead or, at the very least, comatose. The Mansion at Mystic Isle was still at least five miles away by way of pavement, but if we cut across, we could shave four miles off that distance.

Whining like spoiled ten-year-olds, we locked up George's albatross, left it on the side of the road, and set out on foot. Thank God we were in our comfortable shoes.

The bayou at night is about as hospitable as a cemetery on Halloween. And that particular night, with a light wind rustling the trees and bushes and clouds blacking out the moon, the woods around Mystic Isle were probably even worse than that—at least according to Cat.

"You know what they say 'bout the bayou at night?"

"Yes," I said, sighing. "You've told me." At least a dozen times. New Orleanians can be a superstitious lot, Cat way more than I. "That's just a boogeyman story people tell their kids to scare them into being good."

"Uh-huh. It's Rougarou."

"Right." I was out of breath. Slogging through the swamp was tiring. "Didn't you tell me you saw it one time?"

"Not me," she said, her voice quivering. "Quincy."

That explains it.

"He told me he saw that big ol' thing one night under the full moon. Quincy said the Rougarou was eating a chicken."

I glanced sideways at her, but in the dark I couldn't tell if she was kidding or not. "Chicken?"

"That's what he said."

"Did he say it was Southern-fried, fricasseed, or roasted?"

"Mel," she whispered, "don't make fun. It's bad juju."

It was the one thing about Cat that made me a little bit crazy. She knew every creepy story about every creepy thing ever said about Louisiana. And believe me, there were plenty of them. She and Grandmama Ida could (and did) sit up all night sometimes talking about ghoulies and ghosties and long-leggedy beasties, and things that go bump in the night.

I didn't buy into all that spooky talk—much. But it was pretty dark out there, and who knew what all those weird noises were? I took pity on Cat and pulled out my cell phone and switched on the flashlight just for her benefit though, just so *she* wouldn't be so scared.

And it seemed to work for a while. She quit talking about the Rougarou and walked boldly along beside me—until the battery gave it up, and we were out in the middle of friggin' nowhere in pitch dark, listening to the sounds of the wind rustling the cypress trees and water slapping against their trunks.

Things croaked and squawked. I'd be lying if I said that after a while it didn't get to me too. We clutched each other and crept along through the wetlands barely able to see each other, much less anything beyond that.

The operative words were *creeped out*, and it didn't help when something grunted nearby, then hissed, then growled, and Cat shrieked, "Ohmigod, what is that?"

Suddenly it was scary as hell, the air humid and thick, mist floating around our feet, the soft ground sucking at our shoes, while tendrils of the trees grazed our skin like the trailing fingers of witches sizing us up like Hansel and Gretel for a late-night snack.

"Oh, and what was that?" Cat whirled, nearly knocking me down in her panic.

I'd heard it too. "I don't know." I squinted into the darkness.

"Let's go," she said, turning back around.

We picked up our pace, walking faster, trying not to step off solid ground into a bog that might swallow us up to the waist.

A banshee-like wail pushed the two of us closer together. My breathing was as hard and fast as hers.

Whatever we'd sensed behind us was still there, coming, and keeping up. And then whatever it was seemed to multiply. The rustling and sounds of movement expanded, like stereo, spreading from behind us to all around.

"How big did Q say that Rougarou was?"

Without another word, we began to shuffle along even faster. The sounds were closer, the scurrying of some ungodly, nameless thing pursuing us through the dark, around the fallen trees and dangerous holes.

Slugging it out through the mud now, we moved faster, at a run. I was near to crying, and thought I heard a sob from Cat too.

And then she wasn't beside me anymore.

I stopped, frozen to the spot like a statue. "Cat? Where are you?"

"Uh," she groaned. "Down here."

"Oh, lordy." I bent down and helped her to her feet. "What happened?"

"It was that gol'danged big tree root." She tried to kick it but shrieked instead and went down again.

In the dark, I couldn't see anything except her outline. Her hands moved to her ankle. "Damn it, Mel. I don't think I can walk."

"Really?" I looked around frantically, like that would help. "I guess I could go for—"

"Don't you even think about leaving me, missy. Here. Give me a hand."

With my pulling and her pushing, we managed to get her on her feet just as more rustling from the bushes posed a new threat.

"Oh, man." I whimpered.

The clouds parted, and I could see her face now, the whites of her eyes huge and luminous. I was pretty sure mine were just as big.

Something behind seemed to lunge at us from the darkness.

"Oh, crap!" I screamed.

Up ahead, we could see the lights from The Mansion peeking through the trees. We were close. Could we make it before whatever was after us caught up?

"Rougarous are partial to chicken, right?" An illustrated image of the big, ugly man-beast thing popped into my mind. What I seemed to remember most about the Rougarou were its big teeth and razor-sharp talons.

Leaning heavily on me, she began to hobble alongside. We weren't moving very fast, and it certainly wasn't easy going—but at least we were putting up a good fight. No way in hell I was going to be eaten by that swamp monster. Winding up as some creature's hot lunch wasn't how I pictured ending my days.

My heart screamed in my chest. Terror clawed at my throat. Whatever it was closed in.

Then bam!

I ran straight into something, tall and warm and hard.

It moved. I screamed. Cat struck out.

"Ouch!"

Huh?

"Melanie? Is that you? Miss Gabor?"

Oh, thank God.

My voice shook. "Cap'n Jack?"

There was no immediate reply, then, "Uh, yeah. I guess."

It hit me then. In my panic, I'd just called my boss by my pet name for him. How the hell was I going to explain that?

* * *

Turned out it was a pack of those ugly twenty-pound swamp rats curious about the two of us girls wandering around in the bayou—not the Rougarou. If we'd just turned around and yelled at them, they probably would have scattered like cue balls on the first break. But no, we decided to run like sissies. How embarrassing.

Not to mention we'd made so much racket, the resort's general manager had to come out to see what all the racket was about.

As a reward for his concern, my best friend hit him in the nose.

And then to top it all off, the pièce de résistance, I called him, *dear Lord say it isn't so*, Cap'n Jack. The fact that it had started to rain again seemed irrelevant in the face of such disaster as that.

CHAPTER SIX

———

It was after midnight, officially Tuesday morning, by the time I iced Cat's sprained ankle and found an Ace bandage to wrap it. We'd headed straight for one of the housekeeping lounges because there was easy access to the hallway ice machines. I finally located one that wasn't on the blink and filled up a plastic pail that Cat put her sore foot in for about fifteen minutes.

I was in the process of wrapping it for her when Jack showed up with an elegant mahogany cane. "Mr. Villars left it in my office the other day," he explained.

That made sense. Harry Villars was such a clotheshorse, everything, even down to the cane, was an accessory to him. Harry always seemed to be dressed to the nines in three-piece suits, both summer and winter, patterned *real* bow ties, pastel leather moccasins, and a straw Panama hat. He usually made sure the hatband matched the bow tie and pocket square. He wouldn't consider himself fully dressed without the cane to help his strut, and I was surprised he hadn't returned right away for it. Then again, he probably had twenty or thirty more in his closet at *la petite maison*.

Cat took the cane gingerly. "Thank you. I'll be exceptionally careful with it, and if I'm not much better tomorrow, I'll find some crutches so you can return this to him."

Jack took a chair, turned it around, and straddled it. He rubbed a hand across his stubbled jaw. I wanted to do that too—run my hand across his stubbled jaw, not mine. If I was honest, my jaw was never stubbled. "So, ladies," he began, looking first at Cat then at me. "Do you want to tell me what you were doing out in the middle of the swamp this time of night?"

Cat ducked her head and took a long time studying the handle of the cane.

When the coward didn't speak, I cleared my throat. That was all, just cleared my throat. I mean, what could I say to him?

After a minute, I went with the truth. "It was my idea. Cat just came along because I hounded her until she agreed to. It's all about Fabrizio. They took him away. To jail." My voice broke. "He's like family to me. I just wanted to..."

I couldn't go on. The idea of poor Fabrizio sitting in jail all alone just broke my heart.

Jack, bless his gorgeous heart, seemed to understand. "You were just trying to help him. Weren't you?"

I nodded, not trusting myself to speak.

"And you thought, what? That maybe by coming back here, you'd find something that would clear him and lead the investigation in another direction?"

"Oh." I was stunned. "You get it."

He nodded.

And I didn't even really have to explain. I was right—we *were* soul mates.

"And," he went on, "with Miss Gabor out of commission, you'll need someone to watch out for you while you're investigating."

Was he saying what I thought he was saying? I held my breath. It was too much to hope for.

"I mean, we could be dealing with a desperate character here. You could be in danger."

Something warm opened up inside me, like a flower blooming in the sun.

"And I owe it to Mr. Villars to try and clear Fabrizio. It's detrimental to the resort to have an employee charged with a crime of this magnitude. But," he went on, "no matter what we decide to do, we need to be fully cognizant of our guests' privacy. We wouldn't want Mr. Villars to be served a harassment lawsuit. Would we?"

The flower wilted. It was beginning to sound as if clearing Fabrizio was secondary to making sure I didn't step on anyone's toes while I was doing it. It looked like Jack Stockton was all about business after all.

But Fabrizio needed me, and my confidence level was too shallow to believe I could do this by myself, so I took what I could get. "Thank you, Jack," I said. "It's kind of you to offer to help."

While we hadn't intended to stay overnight again, it just seemed to work out that way. Our old room hadn't been booked, and Jack didn't seem to mind that we were back. I wanted to think it was because he was so taken with me he couldn't stand the thought of my being far away. Fantasy aside, I think he was just being nice.

He walked us to our room. Cat thanked him for all his help and swore that something as inconsequential as a sore ankle wouldn't keep her from her post at the table in her shop, The House of Cards. The only equipment she needed to pull the wool over the eyes of her customers was a table, a couple of chairs, and of course a deck of tarot cards. Her workplace was small in space but big on atmosphere. Villars himself had decorated it in the flamboyant manner of a gypsy caravan. It was exotic and attractive in a wild sort of way, just like Catalina herself.

Leaning on Harry's cane, she went in the room, leaving Jack and me standing in the hallway. We were at least a foot apart, but it felt like inches. I swear his body was throwing off heat. My mouth went dry.

"What's your work schedule for tomorrow, Miss…Melanie?"

"I have two appointments, but I should be done by two or two-thirty in the afternoon."

He smiled and nodded. "Let's get together after that then and get organized."

"Organized?"

"Yes, of course. We can't just go off in every direction, not if we hope to exonerate Fabrizio in a timely manner."

Really? Couldn't he just say, "We need to make a plan, girl"?

But instead of making that suggestion, I said, "Great idea, Jack."

We stood there a moment longer in uncomfortable silence.

"Well, then, I guess I'll see you tomorrow afternoon," he said, turning away.

"Right," I said, resisting the urge to salute. "Tomorrow afternoon."

"Sleep well." His voice trembled a little. What was that about?

"Yes, you too." I reached for the door handle.

He stopped. "Melanie?"

"Sir?"

He looked back over his shoulder, a bewildered look on his face. "Earlier. Did you call me Cap'n Jack?"

I nearly choked. "Cap'n...?" Oh, he did hear me. "Why, no."

He smiled.

Dang. I've always been a terrible liar. "Cap'n Jack? Why would I call you that?"

"That's what I was wondering myself. Good night, Melanie." And he walked away.

Cat was already in bed, her foot propped on a pillow. She didn't look happy.

"Does it hurt?" I asked.

She shrugged. "A little, nothing major, but I doubt I'll be much help to you unless there's some real improvement by tomorrow."

She seemed so down I took pity on her. "Don't worry about it, Cat. Getting to the bottom of this should be a fairly simple matter. Don't you think?"

She just looked at me. "Simple? What makes you say that?"

"Well, not that many people knew about the money. Right? So, all we have to do is figure out who needed it the most. On TV, it's usually the person with the best motive."

She nodded slowly. "And on TV that person doesn't stop at stealing. On TV, there's always a homicide."

We looked at each other, and it wasn't even necessary to say it, but I did anyway. "Like the homicide that happened here, like maybe the murderer was after the money all along."

"That's right," she said, "and I'm hoping Quincy doesn't make that connection before we can find out who really took all that money and framed Fabrizio."

It hit me then. "You think Quincy's trying to pin the murder on Fabrizio too?"

She gave me a look. "Mel, he so much as said so."

A wave of anger washed through me. "What's wrong with that boyfriend of yours, anyway? He must be some kind of bully to go after a helpless older guy like Fabrizio. How can you be with someone like that?"

Cat looked stunned. "Bully? Mel, it's his job. Someone was murdered, and he's just trying to see poor Mrs. Elway gets justice."

Okay. So, yes, I was being unreasonable. But my friend was in jail. I staunchly supported my own theory he was innocent and had been set up, and Deputy Quincy Boudreaux was a good target for my anger. "Well, he just oughta back off."

Cat's voice was on the rise too. "Back off? What the heck are you talking about? He can't back off. He's the law."

I didn't want to fight with her. And as much as I didn't want to admit it, she was right. But I was scared for my friend. And I didn't see the sheriff's office making it a point to look beyond Fabrizio for a suspect.

"I just hope Quincy doesn't find anything to make him think it was Fabrizio who fooled with those clams."

Cat didn't look at me when she said, "I don't suppose you've considered that maybe the entity who tainted those clams that killed Mrs. Elway might not be among the living."

I snorted. "Yeah. Right."

But she looked so serious, it gave me pause.

"It was a séance, *chère*," she went on. "There were more beings in that room than the seven living, breathing ones."

"Oh, come on, Cat. You don't really think Fabrizio could have conjured up a spirit? I mean, Fabrizio? He's about as real as those knock-off Rolexes they sell down on street corners in the Quarter."

But Cat wasn't so easy to convince. "You just ask your grandmama, Mel. She'll tell you. If a ghost has an axe to grind,"—nice turn of phrase, don't you think?—"he can cross back over. No problem. I think it was Theodore Elway himself who did the old girl in."

I really wish she hadn't said that. Even someone as sensible as I could get the heebie-jeebies when you started talking about spooks on a rampage.

"Go to sleep, Cat. You're giving me the shivers."

She shook one finger at me knowingly, lay back, and switched off the lamp.

I tried to stop the crazy thoughts running rampant through my poor, tired brain. Vengeful ghosts. I replayed the séance scene in my head. It was true. The door was shut, and nobody went in or out. Light from the hallway would have bled if the door was opened. Either the clams had to have been poisoned before I brought them into the room or someone brought the toxin to the party and dumped it on when things got a little crazy as Fabrizio conjured up the spirit of Mr. Elway. Or, maybe Cat was right. Maybe the phantom reached out from beyond the grave and knocked off his widow.

Maybe she should have brought the hot sauce after all.

Lots of maybes.

Somewhat lulled by the sound of rain spattering the window, I drifted off into a troubled sleep, strange visions filling my head.

For no apparent reason, I jerked awake. What caused it? Was there a noise? Did something move?

The portrait of Alphonse Villars was bathed in eerie night shine coming through the window. The rivulets of rain on the window reflected on the glass and made it appear as if tears ran down Alphonse's face. But what really bothered me was that it hung at an odd angle.

Had it been that way when I went to sleep? I couldn't be sure, but I didn't think so. Unable to resist, I got out of bed and crossed the room to straighten it.

Back in bed, I rolled over. But turned back at a high-pitched sound like fingernails scraping along a blackboard. Alphonse was cockeyed again. *What's up with that?* I refused to believe anything supernatural was going on. I obviously hadn't centered it when I straightened it the first time.

Cat's breathing was soft and even. It seemed Alphonse's gyrations hadn't bothered her. Not so, *moi*. I got out of bed a second time and tilted the portrait back to even. I stood there a couple of minutes, waiting to see if it was going to slide off-center yet a third time. When nothing happened, I padded back across the room and got back into bed.

I was just drifting off again when the most God-awful crash brought me straight up out of bed and onto my feet. This time Cat didn't sleep through it.

"What the heck was that?" she yelped.

"I believe Harry's ancestor is trying to tell us something."

Cat switched on the bedside lamp.

The portrait had fallen (or was yanked) completely off the wall this time.

It lay face down on the floor. Other than the levitating painting, everything else in the room seemed normal.

I got out of bed a third time, lifted the heavy painting, and carried it to the closet, slid it inside, shut the door. For good measure, I slid a chair up against the closet door.

"Take that, Alphonse," I said, crawling back into bed. "You spend some time in the locker, old boy."

Cat rolled over and looked at me before she reached to turn off the lamp. "Maybe Alphonse Villars has been hanging with Theodore Elway."

CHAPTER SEVEN

————

I closed down Dragons and Deities at two forty Tuesday afternoon, later than I expected due to an unfortunate clog in one of my ink guns, which held me up about twenty minutes while I changed to another. I used the privacy screen to change out of my costume into a pair of crop pants and a camp shirt, locked the door, hung the closed sign, and scurried—like one of those awful swamp rats chasing us the night before—to the Presto-Change-o Room, where Jack sat waiting on a barstool.

After I banished Alphonse Villars to the closet, I'd slept like a baby and was feeling pretty good.

Jack was going to help me in my quest to get Fabrizio out of jail. It was as if a huge load had been lifted off my shoulders. Cat had good intentions and all, but I didn't think blaming the homicide on a pissed-off specter was going to be much help to Fabrizio. Besides, Deputy Quincy Boudreaux was a force of nature, and if he figured out that Cat was trying to dip her toe into his case, it would be like two storm fronts converging when they butted heads. This way she didn't have to worry about it, and I got to spend time with the rakish and intrepid Cap'n Jack.

My last thought before walking into the Presto-Change-o Room was, *I can't believe I called him Cap'n Jack to his face.*

* * *

The Presto-Change-o Room was a combination bar and restaurant. It took the place of a coffee shop in the morning, a café during the day, a restaurant in the evening, and a club at night. Blues and jazz bands were often brought in to liven the place up on Friday and Saturday. The walls were a combination of wood painted turquoise with bright-yellow accents, and heavily stained oak around the bar and back bar. Tables with red-and-white checked tablecloths were set up all around a big open dance floor. Art posters of Louisiana food and drink lined the walls. At the far end of the room, a mural with a "Cajun" magician pulling a gator out of a hat covered the whole wall behind the bandstand.

Jack had changed from his suit to a pair of khaki twills, a navy T-shirt, and pair of navy boat shoes. I'd never seen him dressed that way before. He was always Mr. Manhattan in his expensive business suits. But this way, he looked more like the buccaneer of my fantasies. The T-shirt showed off his tanned arms and fit like a glove, clinging to his lean torso and broad shoulders. The man somehow even managed to make khakis look good. It was going to be hard to concentrate on the investigation with him hanging around looking more delish than my grandmama's pecan pie with whipped cream on top. But I'd muddle through somehow.

He swiveled on his stool when I walked up. "Hello." He managed to make it sound like, "Come with me to the Kasbah." I would have gone even if I didn't know where or what the Kasbah actually was. "Did you take time for lunch yet?"

I shook my head.

He picked up his drink, a tall iced tea with a sprig of mint, and led me to a nearby empty table, where he pulled out a chair and handed me a menu before sitting down across from me.

Such a sweetie.

When I expressed my preference for the crabmeat po'boy, he hopped up out of his chair, went to the bar, and put the order in. Couldn't ask for better service.

I admired the rear view as he stood waiting, chin resting on one hand, one foot resting on the footrail.

At the far end of the bar, a middle-aged guy with fairly new hair plugs, wearing a pair of cargo pants and a golf shirt, was reading the riot act to the bartender, a new hire I hadn't met yet, probably hired on because he was the right fit for the wizard costume. "My wife says this wine sucks! It's gone to vinegar. What the hell you gonna do about it?"

The bartender's smile never flagged. "I'm sorry for the inconvenience, sir. Let me get your wife a fresh pour."

The man obviously seemed to feel a fresh pour wouldn't do the trick, because he flung the wine on the bartender's wizard robes. In my book, that was like a slap in the face. It would cost a heckuva lot to dry-clean that outfit.

Jack ambled over to the irate guest. "I couldn't help overhearing, sir. Is there—"

Mr. Generally Pissed Off sized up Jack then blurted, "Mind your own beeswax, pretty boy."

Jack nodded, a look of contemplation on his face. "Beeswax, eh?" The man thrust out his chin, while Jack just ran a hand over his own. "I like that word a lot. You wouldn't mind if I use it myself every now and then, would you?"

Good old Pissed Off stared at Jack for a beat, two—then he smiled—then he laughed. "No sir, I reckon you can use that word all you like, mister. No charge, either."

The two shook hands then Jack said, "My name's Stockton. Jack Stockton. I'm the hotel's general manager. How about you let us buy you and your wife a new bottle, and we'll make sure there's no charge for the first one."

Mr. Generally Pissed Off seemed to like that idea. He clapped Jack on the back and headed off to a table by one of the windows.

Jack and the bartender shared one of those moments of relief—a problem had been averted, and without bloodshed too.

That was Jack's way. He seemed to take everything in stride. And it wasn't the first time I'd seen him take lemons and make Arnold Palmers.

When he returned, he mentioned he'd made arrangements for George's poor old Volvo to be towed back to the dock and had called George to let him know.

While I waited for my sandwich, it seemed like a good idea to launch a plan.

I couldn't help leaning on my elbow and staring at him—dreamy eyed, I'm sure. "What did you have in mind?" Those probably weren't the best words, but he didn't seem to notice. Looked as if I was the only one at the table who heard a double entendre.

"Me? I'm the sidekick, remember? Watson to your Sherlock?"

Oh, right. "Well…" I began then stopped. Maybe I was more like Inspector Clouseau than Sherlock Holmes. "Okay. The cops took Fabrizio because they said they found a lot of cash hidden in his room. Right?"

He nodded.

"And they *couldn't* find the hundred grand this Terrence guy told them Mrs. Elway brought with her."

Another nod. He leaned forward and rested his chin on his fist. I sighed, lost my train of thought, and had to look down at my hands to get it back. "So I was thinking maybe we ought to follow the money."

He looked up at the ceiling a while then smiled. "Brilliant."

That was when it occurred to me that the money might also have something to do with Cecile Elway's death, and that maybe if we figured out who took the money, we might also figure out who killed the old girl.

I said so, and that made Jack smile. "Hmm, elementary, my dear Sherlock."

I smiled back. "Isn't that my line? But, where do we start?"

"You were there. Why don't you tell me what you remember."

I began at the beginning and ended with, "The door was locked. As far as I know, no one went out or came in once the séance began." Thinking about it gave me the shivers. "Golly, Jack, if I didn't know she was murdered, I'd say she died from natural causes…" It just popped into my head and out of my mouth before I thought about it. "Or maybe supernatural causes."

* * *

After I scarfed down the po'boy—and by the way, if you ever stop over at The Mansion at Mystic Isle, I highly recommend you give one a try. It's the kind of food that makes you want to stand up in church and testify—we headed out to the tennis courts where Jack said Terrence Montague, the tagalong *friend* of the victim, had an appointment with the resort tennis pro.

It had rained all the previous night and well into midday, but it looked as if the weather gods had taken pity on Terrence and cleared things up just in time for his tennis lesson. From my perspective, the gods would have been kinder to conjure up a thunderstorm and keep him off the court.

We stood and watched the fiasco for about fifteen or twenty minutes. While Terrence looked sleek in his white shorts and polo, he got around the court like a hippopotamus. He even tripped on his own shoelace once. When he held up his hands and his racquet in surrender, by my clock he still had ten minutes left on his lesson.

Panting like a sixteen-year-old with a pinup of Jennifer Aniston, he bent and placed his hands on his thighs, sucking in deep breaths. "Ah, my dear." He straightened and smiled at our gorgeous blonde two-time French Open–winner tennis pro, a big draw for the resort. "In my opinion the best strategy is to regroup and live to fight another day. It would seem tennis isn't my game." He wiped the sweat from his brow so dramatically, I truly believed it was something he might have practiced in front of a mirror.

Jack and I approached him. He looked up at us in question as he gathered his jacket and bag and prepared to leave the court. "Mr. Stockton," he said pleasantly. There was a hint of the Northeast in his accent, Connecticut maybe, some Yankee state anyway. "How nice to see you again." He turned to me. "Miss…"

"Melanie, Mr. Montague," I said. "You can call me Melanie."

"Excellent, and I'll be Terrence."

Right. Because you are.

Jack took pity on Terrence's beet-red face in spite of the cloud cover and suggested we take our conversation to a shady table on the courtyard terrace outside the Presto-Change-o Room.

Iced teas were ordered and delivered almost immediately to our table. Something to be said for being in the company of the hotel manager, something besides the eye candy aspect.

Jack began, "We were hoping you'd have time to talk to us a little about the tragedy in the séance room."

"Oh." Terrence set his iced tea back on the table and leveled his eyes at Jack. "You mean Cecile's..." He hung his head.

Terrence's face was lean, his jaw square. There was something about him that reminded me of a wolf, hungry—something about the set of his jaw, the undisguised steel in his hazel eyes behind the heavy-rimmed glasses. He lifted a hand to push a lock of light-brown hair off his forehead. His posture stiffened, and for a moment he seemed a different kind of man, someone more shrewd, calculating. Then he relaxed and took another deep pull on the tea.

"Of course, I'm at your disposal," he said in that offhanded way a professor announces a pop quiz.

"How well did you know Cecile Elway?" Like Jack said, it was my investigation, so I decided to get this show on the road.

"Ah," Terrence breathed softly. "Cecile was like a guardian angel, watching over my little friends, the Lepidoptera Alien Caterpillars. The little fellows were the glue binding me and my Cecile together." He shook his head sadly. "Now what will they do? How will they survive without her?"

And without her checkbook, I thought. And now that he'd brought it up, I had to ask. "Did you know her well? Were the two of you—you know?" I gulped, hoping my investigation didn't carry me across the line of acceptable conversation with a paying guest. Couldn't afford to lose my job.

Cap'n Jack came to my rescue—again. "Romantically involved?"

Terrence hesitated and seemed to be considering his answer. "We were indeed. Cecile was a breath of fresh air in a world of toxic fumes. How could I not love her?" *And her wealth? Good old fresh air Cecile Elway.* "She had so much to offer." *Yes. We heard—a few hundred million or so.* "How will I ever manage without her?"

"And what did you get out of the relationship?" Even I cringed. I shouldn't have dropped out of Subtlety 101 midsemester.

"She was a lonely woman. I was a lonely man. We offered each other companionship. We were in love. We were going to get married."

Terrence looked to be around forty. I would have said Cecile was sixty if she was a day, and that was putting it kindly. I would have thought Rosalyn, Cecile's stepdaughter, would have been more to his liking, age-wise that is. But you never knew what would turn a man's head unless you listened to my grandmama, who'd told me on more than one occasion the way to a man's heart was through his wallet. And Cecile was certainly quite alluring in that way.

According to Terrence, Cecile had brought more than one hundred thousand dollars with her to spur the Great Fabrizio to the highest heights of his abilities. Terrence swore he tried to talk her out of coming down here to "this godforsaken swamp."

Godforsaken? Really? Them's fightin' words.

"But she was determined that she needed to make peace with Theodore before we were married, and for some reason had it in her head Fabrizio was the only man who could get the job done." When she died, it had occurred to Terrence someone should locate the cash, so he mentioned it to Deputy Quincy.

"Mr. Montague," Jack said slowly. I knew how carefully he chose his words, making a supreme effort to avoid insulting a resort guest. "Did Mrs. Elway ever discuss the circumstances surrounding her husband's death?"

Terrence didn't answer right away. He just looked at Jack, and I immediately thought about what Rosalyn said in the séance room. "Daddy, tell us. How did you really die? Did someone murder you?"

When Terrence's answer came, it was cryptic and terse. "I don't know why you'd ask me such a question."

"Well, I—"

Terrence interrupted. "As far as I'm aware, Mr. Elway's demise was due to a sudden heart attack, in less delicate terms referred to as a widow-maker. I believe at one point she said he was under a great deal of stress."

Jack and I glanced at each other, both obviously asking ourselves why a multimillionaire would be under all that much stress. But we never had the chance to ask, as Terrence stood and brought our interview to a close. "Now, if you don't mind, I need to leave. Everyone has been raving about the European-style spa here. I made an appointment for a deep-tissue massage, which I'm late for already. And, besides, I assure you I've told you everything I know."

That remained to be seen, but we couldn't hog-tie him, put him under a bright light, and grill him. At least not yet.

Terrence excused himself, leaving Jack and me alone at the table.

It was late afternoon by then, closing in on evening. The thunderclouds that had rolled in nearly blotted out the setting sun completely. The air was thick. There was barely a breeze to cut through the humidity. It was like swamp soup.

The sound system music floated out from the bar. "Witchy Woman." I smiled, remembering that when Jack first came onboard, he had the brilliant idea for him and Harry to put their heads together and compile a themed playlist of songs relating to all things supernatural. It was played at low volume throughout the main building, a bit louder in the bar and restaurant areas. I couldn't tell you how many of my clients commented on it.

Jack laced his fingers behind his head and leaned back in his chair, stretching the knit of his T-shirt tight across his abdomen, his six-pack clearly defined.

He sat forward. "Six what?"

Had I really been counting out loud? I was losing it. "Six of one, half a dozen of the other?"

CHAPTER EIGHT

———

It began to rain again, you know, like cats and dogs, except in the bayou it was gators and bullfrogs. It had been a really wet week.

Cat wasn't scheduled to close up shop yet, so I was at loose ends for an hour or so until dinner. Jack walked me back to my hotel room.

We didn't talk, and it was a bit uncomfortable. I was aware of how tall he was, walking beside me, and his body heat was giving me hot flashes. I kept trying to think of something sophisticated and witty to say, but nothing came to mind.

We stopped outside my door. He looked down at me. I looked up at him and caught my breath. We stood close together. If either of us swayed forward, he bent down, and I stood on my tiptoes, our lips might meet. Okay, so I was really reaching. The picture filled my mind, and I was momentarily lost in the glow.

He cleared his throat. "So, what do we do next?"

"Oh." He probably wasn't speaking of the next move I had in mind. "You mean in our..."

He grinned. "Our investigation."

I ducked my head. "Well, I'm not sure. I guess look up the next person on our interview list."

At that moment, a bone-rattling scream pierced the air.

We both jerked then turned as one and ran back up the hall the way we'd come.

As we entered the main lobby, the desk manager on duty ran up. "Mr. Stockton. Thank God. We've been looking for you. There's an emergency on the property."

Jack frowned. "Emergency? What kind of emergency? Who was screaming? Is someone hurt?"

The front desk man, a recent hire whose acquaintance I hadn't taken the time to make yet, turned and lifted his hands helplessly. Behind him, on the floor beside the check-in counter, the staff groundskeeper and head of maintenance, a huge man named Odeo Fournet, was on his knees in a muddy puddle, crying like a bride left standing at the altar.

Jack rushed to his side and helped him to his feet. "Odeo, what is it? Tell me."

"They's rising up." The white of Odeo's eyes shone like flashlight beams in his ebony face. His tears left crusty tracks down his cheeks. His nose ran. All in all, he looked like he'd fallen in a big hole. "On their own, Mr. Stockton, on their own."

Jack looked at me like maybe I had a clue, which I didn't. I shrugged. "Show me," he said to Odeo, who took Jack's hand in his bigger, grimier one and headed out the front entrance.

I followed along behind them. I had to know. If someone said, "They's rising up," you'd go see what the heck he was talking about, too.

* * *

The Villars family boneyard was on a slight rise not far to the rear of the public areas. Every employee of the resort was required to know the history of the property, and I was no exception.

The Villars clan had first settled in the area under French rule in the mid-1700s. The family had somehow managed to hang on to the land throughout the turbulent Louisiana history until, of course, it was handed over to Harry Villars, our charming but inept leader. Over the centuries, many family members had been interred in the fenced-in cemetery on the crest of that hill. But none in the last fifty years or so due to the ever-rising water table.

The week before, it had rained for two solid days. The levees in town rose. The bayou too. The runoff soaked in, and the water table rose. That was the way of the Mississippi Delta. You dug down a few feet, and you hit water. That was why most of our dearly departed were interred above ground, in big stone tombs. Floating bodies were bad for the tourist trade.

As it was, our dead got shuffled around quite a bit anyway. The way to make room for the recently passed in the family tomb was to move the current occupant to a bone bag, relocate him to the back, and deposit the next unfortunate soul's coffin in the tomb. It was our way. Not good. Not bad. Just our way, and as a general rule, it kept the bodies from floating downstream.

I never imagined it was very popular with those who actually resided inside the tombs, crowded and all, and they never could know when or if they were going to get relocated. Such a transitory afterlife might be one explanation for the restless spirits said to roam Crescent City.

It was obvious all the rain from late the week before had caused the water table to rise and the coffins to make an appearance. The shadows were lengthening, and the rain had momentarily let up, but from looks of the gloomy sky, not for long. The air cooled. The critters were coming out for the day's last serenade, and birdcalls, the croak of frogs, and the buzz of swarms of insects rose all around us.

I've never been a big fan of cemeteries, although those in the city were quite beautiful and serene. I've visited many times to sketch and ponder the rows of magnificent tombs—in the daytime. Never at night. I may be ignorant, but I'm not stupid.

Jack stood on the crest of the hill, hands on his hips. He looked as good from the back as he did from the front—maybe better. Since I was all about that bass.

I trudged up to stand beside him. It was impossible to miss the devastation. Several of the graves had popped open, the coffins, as Odeo accurately said, had "risen up."

The look on Jack's face would have been comical if it weren't so full of horror and astonishment. "What the hell?" he said. "So, let me see if I have this right. It rains—a lot. The water table rises and pushes against the old coffins. And they pop up above ground, scaring the holy crap out of everyone."

I nodded. "Pretty much."

He turned, and in the fading light I could see his bemused expression. "Don't y'all hate it when that happens?" His drawl was a near dead-on imitation of Harry Villars, Southern gentleman extraordinaire.

"I dunno," I said. "If you ask me, this is the kind of thing Harry Villars hopes for. Fits right in with the motif here."

He agreed. "It does."

I can only imagine how this scene must have looked to him.

Big cast stone and concrete grave covers had slid to the side like they were made of Styrofoam. Some cracked. Others broke clean in half. Mud banks pushed up against them. A few of the coffins had been shoved out of the ground by the rising water table to sit crossways over the opening. One poor soul had been deposited a good ways from his resting place—the coffin tipped on its side, the lid stood open. I didn't look too closely at that one.

Another coffin had slid halfway down the hill, stopped from going farther by a crumbling marble grave marker.

It was somewhat of a disaster.

Jack shook himself and took charge. "Odeo, we're gonna need a couple of men with strong backs and a good deal of intestinal fortitude. Also a forklift." He took a long look at the clouds gathering overhead. "Sandbags too, lots of them. The weatherman said we're due for another downpour—if not tonight, tomorrow for certain."

Odeo nodded. "On my way, Mr. Stockton." He turned and moved a few steps away before turning back. "I know where there's a forklift, and I know a couple of guys in maintenance who can give us a hand, but sandbags? I don't..." He lifted his hands, palms up.

"I know where to go," I said. "Odeo, send a couple of your guys to meet me at the boathouse down by the dock."

Jack took hold of his shirt hem and pulled the T-shirt off over his head. Oh, my. I knew I was staring, but who wouldn't?

He draped his shirt over a fence post. I couldn't help but notice how the muscles in his back rippled when he did. It was going to be entertaining to watch the restoration of the Villars Cemetery. Too bad it was getting dark.

Jack turned around and offered me a different viewpoint. His chest and abdomen were smooth, his skin tan, the muscles defined. The six-pack I'd seen earlier through the knit of the T-shirt didn't disappoint in the flesh.

"Miss Hamilton?" he said softly.

My gaze lifted to his face. His eyes were amused, aware. "Mel?"

"Yes?" This time I caught myself before saying Cap'n Jack.

"Sandbags?" He smiled.

I punctuated with my index finger. "Right. Sandbags."

Before I turned away, he took a step and sank up to his knee in mud but didn't seem to mind. Within only a minute, he was straining to lift one of the coffin lids. Already covered in mud, he looked like a man who was actually used to getting his hands dirty. It was a pretty good guess he probably never had to do anything quite like this in NYC, and his willingness to get down and dirty side by side with his team was one of the things that made Jack a really good manager—and I was thinking he was also a really good man.

* * *

Word was that the boathouse was leftover from a time back in the early '90s when the family was trying to raise money by giving guided airboat tours of the Barataria Preserve. When Harry did the repurpose, it became a place where the resort mechanics could work on boats and other equipment, as well as a general storage facility. Sandbags were always kept there in case of floods.

Cat had told me about the building in great detail. One day Quincy needed an extra set of jumper cables. She'd taken him out to the boathouse, and while they were there, they made good use of the sandbags for a bit of a romantic tryst.

When I thought about how Jack Stockton had looked standing on the hill without his shirt, I thought maybe Cat and Quincy had the right idea.

I trotted back to the main building, down to Maintenance in the lower level, located the key labeled *Boathouse* on the pegboard at the back of the room, grabbed it, and headed out the front door.

After sprinting across the circular driveway and lawn, I pushed my way through the copse of low bushes. Ahead of me, the boathouse and wooden dock were visible in the twilight.

I used the key to open the door just as a pickup pulled up with three strapping men in the bed.

They made short work of loading a couple of dozen sandbags, plus a few more for good measure then turned and headed back along the service road around the building to the hilltop graveyard.

I took a second to lock up the boathouse and was just turning to retrace my steps back to the main building to return the key, when the sound of a woman's voice gave me pause.

"What was that all about?"

For some reason I'm still not sure of, I eased back against the wood-shingled wall and listened.

A second voice, male. "Dude, beats me. They sure were in a hurry." Unless my memory failed me, it was Cecile's stepgrandson, Billy.

Something made a slapping sound. "Gosh darn mosquitos." It was Rosalyn, Theodore's daughter, Cecile's stepdaughter. "How can these people stand it? I'm covered in welts."

His voice was disdainful. "Living in the swamp is all these people down here know."

"I suppose." She sighed. "How much longer will they make us stay in this godforsaken mudhole anyway?"

Billy's tone was speculative. "Cat says—"

"Who?"

"You know. Cat, that gypsy girl," he said.

"Oh. That girl, the slutty one."

I was about to step away from the building and confront the old biddy. Nobody dissed my friend and walked away.

But when he went on, I stopped.

"Yeah, that one. Cat says when the sheriff's office knows for sure they have the murderer, they'll let us all go home."

"Really? As if those rubes could even begin to unravel this mess."

"Hmm," Billy snorted. "Mother, I think you might be right for once. Those fools can't even locate the rest of the money Cecile brought down here with her."

The two of them laughed.

The slapping sound came again. "My God, they're eating me alive," Rosalyn whined. "Come along, son. Let's go back to the asylum."

*　*　*

I stayed quiet and still until they'd moved away from the dock and crossed the lawn.

Then, you'd better bet, I made a beeline for the House of Cards upstairs in the main house.

Seven o'clock, and Cat had just locked her shop and was hobbling toward the elevator. She looked up. "Hey."

"You're damn right, 'hey,'" I said. "You'll never guess who I was spying on down by the boathouse just now."

She winked. "Not so hard, girl. Cap'n Jack?"

"Not Jack. He's up on the hill wrestling corpses."

She gave me a look, but before she could open her mouth, I went on.

"It was Rosalyn."

"Cecile's stepdaughter, right?"

I nodded. "And that Billy guy, the stepgrandson."

"Oh." Cat grimaced. "The octopus."

The elevator arrived, the door slid open, and we stepped in.

"They were alone on the dock, and I overheard them talking."

Cat pushed the Lobby button with the tip of her crutch.

"Cat." Something in my voice must have struck a chord with her, because she turned to me, concern in her beautiful brown eyes. "They know a helluva lot more about this than they've let on."

"They do?"

"Yes, and we're going to find out exactly what that is."

"Want me to read their cards?" she asked.

I just looked at her. "Oh. Right. Like that would really help us learn anything."

She shrugged. "You never know."

"Cat, you're not starting to believe all the hype about this place, are you? I mean it's all about as real as...Next thing I know, you'll be believing you're a Disney princess."

She gave me a look, shrugged, and said, "Esmerelda?"

CHAPTER NINE

The Jefferson Parish lockup in the town of Gretna was just on the far side of the ridge forming the river levee. I'd never been there before, a fact of which my mother and grandmama were extremely relieved. In fact, I'd never seen so much barbed wire, concrete, and chain link in my life.

Cat eyed the utilitarian facility coated in industrial grey with a critical eye. "If they painted it a nice yellow or turquoise, it would perk things up some. You think?"

The visitation area had emptied out except for Cat, me, and a stout woman with two small children in tow who kept fooling around with the video equipment and blacking out the screen where the woman seemed to be attempting to have a conversation with a man on the other side. She kept yelling, "Simmer down and get over here and talk to your papa."

The guard on duty schooled the two of us in the "video-visitation" equipment, and before we knew it, we were face-to-screen with the Great Fabrizio.

Poor Fabrizio. Orange was so not his color. It gave his skin a sallow aspect, and his expression was so glum, a grimace would have been an improvement.

Of course, no one really looked all that great in those videoconferences. Grainy, jerky, unsynched displays of shadowed faces distorted by the lens to make a perfectly handsome person look like a bizarre alien. I fully expected him to ask to "phone home."

"How are you holding up?" I asked once he settled down in front of the screen.

"If I am not released forthwith, I believe I shall shrivel up and die." Tears stung my eyes at his sad smile. "Hello, Catalina, my dear," he said.

Her smile was all things at once: sympathy, affection, hope. Cat never had to say much. Her heart was in her eyes, and you could read her soul on her face.

"Thank you for coming to see me," Fabrizio said. "What transport did you find?"

"Quincy came and picked us up at The Mansion," Cat said. "I guess there's something to be said for dating the law after all."

He looked so sad. His long face always had a semi-forlorn look, but now even more than usual.

"We've been trying to figure out who really took that money, Fabrizio, to get you out of this terrible place." I touched the screen. Trying to talk to someone like this was...well...he might as well have been on the moon.

He shook his head as a light from somewhere above him made a halo. "On my oath, Melanie, I knew nothing of a large amount of cash. How can they believe I stole something of which I knew nothing?"

I didn't know what to say to comfort him but had to ask, "Fabrizio?" I lowered my voice to a near whisper. "You told me yourself she was going to pay you a hundred thousand dollars if you succeeded in contacting Mr. Elway on the other side."

"Yes. I knew she was going to pay me. I never said I didn't know anything about the payment. I said I didn't know anything about the cash."

I was really confused now. ""But how did you expect her to pay you?"

He shrugged pathetically. "I thought perhaps a check? Or maybe PayPal?"

One of the children skipped over and stood in front of the camera, waving his little hand directly in front of it. "Hi! Hi!" Too cute. "Ya stinking jailbird." Maybe not as cute as I originally thought. I gave him the evil eye, but he stuck his tongue out at me.

Cat did little more than cock an eyebrow and point her finger. "Go," she said. "Now."

It was like magic. The child sobered and stared at her as he backed away then turned and ran to his mother's side.

I'm telling you, sometimes I just wonder about my girl. She's something else. Grandmama Ida would say she's got the power.

I never was sure exactly what that meant, but if power was what it was, well, Cat did have it.

We continued to talk to him for another fifteen minutes until our session was over. I wished we'd at least been in the same room. Sitting in front of a monitor, talking to a pane of glass, didn't constitute a "visit" in my book.

Quincy walked us out to the parking lot.

"Have you come up with any other suspects?" I asked.

He turned from making bedroom eyes at Cat. "Other suspects, *chère*? Now why would I be looking at other suspects? The man with all that cash stashed away, he in the slammer right now."

"But he didn't—"

He put his index finger against his lips. "Shush."

"But it wasn't even all the—"

He did it again. My dander was up.

"You can't just—"

"Shush now, darlin'. I'll take care of bringing down all dem bad boys, and you take care of makin' pretty pictures on all dem rich folks over at The Mansion."

"Who do you think—"

"Shush."

Dammit. If he did it one more time, I was going to bite off that finger!

"Besides," he bragged, "I already caught me one catfish red-handed. And when the tox screen comes back, I'm pretty darn sure I can connect that same ol' catfish to the homicide of that fancy Yankee lady. First rule of law enforcement, *chère*, follow the money trail, and you'll wind up with a surefire payday."

I sincerely wished he'd stop saying things like that.

There were times I had no earthly idea what Cat saw in Deputy Quincy Boudreaux. Like now. I mean, besides his trim, fit body. The sly confidence that shone out of those big brown peepers. That sweet, self-deprecating grin that melted a girl's heart. He was an out-and-out overly cocky son of the bayou. He must have been really good in bed. Otherwise, why would a woman like Cat put up with that annoying, know-it-all 'tude?

"Are you telling me you're looking to pin a murder on Fabrizio?"

He winked, and it was all I could do not to clock him a good one.

"Ooops." He stopped walking. "I need to go back inside a sec, y'all. You go on to the squad car. I'll catch up." He hurried back inside.

I whirled on Cat. "How can you just stand there and let him say those things?"

"Me? This is my fault? Mel, he's a cop. That's what cops say. Things like, 'Book 'em, Dano,' and 'Freeze, dirtbag.' That's just the way they are. Quincy doesn't mean anything by it."

"You are so naïve. He's going after our friend to lock him up for a million years or maybe even exterminate him like some old swamp rat. Cat, can't you see you gotta do something?"

She just stood there under the yellow glare of the pole light. I could tell by the set of her mouth and the way she blinked her eyes I'd hurt her feelings. I mean, it wasn't her fault her boyfriend was a rat. But I was riled up and not in the mood to take it back.

"So, whatcha goin' to do about it?" I lifted my chin and looked down my nose at her.

She pulled herself up to her impressive height of five foot five (towering a full two inches over me), threw back her slim shoulders, and thrust out her ample bosom. "Well, right now, I'm going to get a ride back to the ferry, go home, and go to bed, and not talk to you 'til you decide to be civil."

She turned and walked away.

"Well, where's she goin'?" Quincy had walked back up behind me.

Okay, so I didn't always play fair. "Well, you made her mad, Quincy. She was just fit to be tied 'bout what you were saying about Fabrizio. She couldn't take it anymore and had to leave."

His jaw dropped open, and he stared after Cat.

Cat stopped a ways down the sidewalk and turned around, giving a thumbs up in our general direction. What the heck was that all about? That was a weird thing to do when she was angry, weird even for Cat.

Oddly, Quincy seemed to understand.

I wasn't done with him yet. "I can't say as I blame her one bit." My voice rose in pitch and volume. "Why, you're just a big ol' meanie." I'm a bit ashamed to tell you I stamped my foot. It was a full-on hissy fit.

His eyes narrowed. His grin faded to a straight line. He took hold of my arm and pulled gently. I got the idea he wanted me to go with him back inside, so I did, still sputtering and fuming.

He talked as we walked along. "You do realize you're speaking to an officer of the law. Right, missy?"

"An officer of the…what the heck are you talking about?"

"I'm talking about someone who's a little out of hand right now, maybe just a little too worked up for her own good. Someone who might've said something she oughtn't have to someone I was hoping to cuddle up to later tonight."

He stopped walking, and I had a look around. We'd gone down a hall or two by now and were in a different section of the building than before. A long counter with a glass partition was the only feature of the room. The door at the end of the long, narrow area was thick steel with a wire-mesh window and a lock that looked like it could withstand a nuclear blast.

"Sergeant Mackelroy?" Quincy said softly.

A female deputy came from around a desk. She had big blue eyes, big blue eyes that looked awfully interested in Deputy Quincy. "Yes, Q? Whatcha'all need?"

He sort of shoved me at her. "This here is a dear friend of mine. She's not feelin' all that well, and I thought maybe we'd be well-advised to find her a nice place to rest awhile."

Sergeant Mackelroy nodded. "I see, Q." What was up with this Q stuff? Cat would certainly be interested to hear about it. "I know just the spot. Come with me, miss."

* * *

I spent almost an hour in the Jefferson Parish lockup. It was humiliating, but the cell was clean and didn't even smell. I didn't have any muscly, Russian wrestler-type roommates, just one little middle-aged woman who'd been brought in for dancing on the tables at Thierry's Crab Shack. She sported a gorgeous running sleeve of wild roses on her right arm and a vine of lush ivy on her left shoulder. By the time I'd exhausted all my good tattoo conversation with her and was just sitting in uncomfortable silence while she threw up in the toilet, Sergeant Mackelroy came and unlocked the door.

She crooked her finger at me, and I walked out.

Even she laughed when I turned in a circle and exulted, "Free at last. Free at last."

That was when the voice from behind me made by blood run cold.

"Funny. I wouldn't have taken you for the hardened criminal sort, Miss Hamilton."

I looked around to where Jack Stockton stood in the open doorway between the lockup area and the front counter.

My first thought was, *well, hell.*

My second was, *aw, what the heck. I've been on worse first dates.*

He said he'd come when Cat called him and told him I was upset about Fabrizio being in the parish lockup and just needed to settle down some. How did she even know about this?

It seemed that Cat had indeed caught a ride back to the ferry then on home to our place in the city. For some reason, she called Jack to come and pick me up.

I rode back to The Mansion with Jack in one of the hotel maintenance pickups. Saying it was a quiet ride was the understatement of the decade. I don't think either of us spoke a word until he parked the truck near the boathouse, and we started to walk back to The Mansion.

It was getting on to midnight. The ferry would have quit running by then, which was a good thing in the end because it would give both Cat and me a chance to cool off. Jack didn't seem to mind me staying at the resort yet another night. In fact, he seemed comfortable with the idea.

He walked me back to what I was beginning to think of as my room.

At the door, I turned to him. I was still pretty embarrassed about the whole thing. "I'm sorry you had to come break me out of the slammer," I said, trying to cast a humorous light on things.

"No big deal, really," he said softly. "Catalina said your visit with the Great Fabrizio left you pretty upset. She said Deputy Boudreaux was just trying to help you, as she put it, 'simmer down some.'"

Simmer down? I needed to have a talk with that girl.

"She also said you're a young woman of high passion with a lot of energy, and that I might consider trying to help you rechannel some of that energy."

I looked up at him. His eyes twinkled. Yes, I said *twinkled*. His mouth was quirked in a small twist of a smile. He lifted a hand to my face and pushed a strand of hair behind my ear. His hand stayed on my cheek. Soft. Warm.

"Rechannel, eh?" I said so softly I barely heard it myself.

He nodded.

I turned my face into his hand.

I swear he shuddered. I did.

But the moment passed without either of us acting further. How could we? He was Cap'n Jack, my boss, a man walking on the eggshell remains of the reputation he brought with him from the Big Apple. And me, I was a female hotel employee. I might as well have been wearing a sign around my neck saying *You can't touch this*.

CHAPTER TEN

———

Mystic Isle was awash in summer drizzle Thursday morning. It was a nice, soft rain. Not the socked-in downpour from previous days. Maybe the coffins would stay in the ground this time. I hoped so for Jack's sake.

My first appointment was at nine thirty, so I showered and dressed then went to Dragons and Deities by way of the employee lounge, where I brewed up a cup of chicory strong enough to grow hair on my chest, and carried it along with an almond bear claw to Dragons and Deities.

I arrived about fifteen minutes early, just enough time to break my fast, as Grandmama Ida would have said, and get set up for the day. Only a short while before the client was scheduled to arrive, Cat appeared with a bag from the Café du Monde. I could smell the beignets from where she stood in the open doorway.

"Peace offering?" She held up the bag.

I laid a towel on top of the bear claw and nodded. "Come on in, *chère*," I said. "How'd you know I was dying for some beignets this morning?"

We made up.

Before she headed off to her own little den to divine the fortunes of the general population, she gave me a hug.

"I hate it when we fight," I said.

She laughed. "You call that fighting? Oh, by the way, Beauregard has to go out of town to visit his sick uncle in Savannah, which means Satchmo is heading on back home tonight."

"So we have to be there."

"Well, one of us does, anyway." Her eyes were kind. "Look, *chère*, I know how much Fabrizio means to you, and I know how bad you're wanting to help him get out of the clinker. I'll travel back and forth like normal to take care of Satchmo and anything else that comes up on the home front. But if you can get Cap'n Jack to agree to it, whyn't you just plan to stay here until you get the Great Fabrizio back where he belongs? I even packed you a bag—all those little things a girl needs when she's roughing it."

Smart thinking on Cat's part. Staying at the resort would make my investigation a whole lot easier.

"So how was your quality time with Cap'n Jack?" Her back was to me as she walked the room, looking at my sample artwork on the walls, but I could tell by the pitch of her voice she was being coy.

It hit me then. "You!" I said. "You set me up, didn't you? The quiet time in the slammer, the ride back to The Mansion? You were playing matchmaker again."

She turned, and from her smug grin, I knew it was true. "It worked, didn't it? You and Cap'n Jack were all cozy on the ride back? Did you…?" She made little kissy noises.

"I can't believe you did that. How the heck did you get Quincy to go along with it?"

She smiled and cupped her hands beneath her breasts. "Me and the girls have our special ways. Let's eat."

The beignets were a work of art. The chicory coffee I'd brewed, divine. The tattoo I designed for my new client, sheer genius.

But throughout the whole morning, all I could think about was getting Fabrizio out of that dismal place. It was obvious, to me anyway, that the law had few, if any, intentions of looking beyond my friend for suspects. Quincy, normally a reasonable, likable guy, had turned into a bullheaded son of a gun who not only intended to see Fabrizio prosecuted for stealing a hundred thousand dollars, he was looking to get him on murder charges too.

That was something I didn't intend to see happen. Toward that end, I used my lunch break to seek out the Elways.

I found Billy first.

I was on my way to his mother's room on the second floor when I saw him go into the House of Cards to see Cat. He was having his fortune read—again. If Cat counted right, this was the sixth time in four days. Wouldn't you think he'd take notes or something? Or at least take a picture of Cat to carry around with him in case any other hotel guests might want to set up an appointment with her.

I hung around in the outer room amusing myself with a copy of *Soothsayers' Journal* while she took him back to her "office" for the reading. When they came out twenty minutes later, Billy looked peeved, and Cat looked fed up.

"Don't y'all forget what I've been telling you, Mr. Whitlock." Cat shook her finger at him. "Stay away from those loose women. They may tell you they're having safe sex, but they don't even know the meaning of the term."

He shrugged and lifted his hands sadly. "I wouldn't need any loose women if you'd just be my woman, Catalina."

"Now, now," she said, hustling him toward the door. In a low-pitched aside, I heard, "Like that's gonna happen before hell freezes over."

I stood. "Billy?"

He looked over, just noticing me.

"I was wondering if maybe you had a minute to talk." When he looked me up and down and grinned, I hurried to add, "I have a few questions about…you know…what happened at the séance Sunday night."

"Sure," he said, tossing a *take that* sort of look in Cat's direction. "How 'bout you buy me a drink?"

We went downstairs to the Presto-Change-o Room, where we sat at the bar and ordered drinks—a hurricane for Billy and a Diet Dr Pepper for me.

He took out the straw and drank it in big gulps. He lifted the empty glass toward the waitress on shift, signaling for another.

"You might want to slow down there, Billy," I said. "Those things'll sneak up on you." It was a mixed bag, wasn't it? I wanted him a little loosey-goosey so he'd tell me what I wanted to know, but at the same time, it didn't seem like a great idea to be the reason a hotel guest had to crawl back to his room.

At least he was taking a little more time with the second cocktail. Maybe I wouldn't have to carry him upstairs after all.

"So, Billy," I began. "Have you heard the police are calling Cecile's death a homicide?"

He licked the red stain of the grenadine off his upper lip, plucked the Maraschino cherry from the glass, and began to suck on it suggestively while staring into my eyes. Really?

"Yeah, I heard. Too bad for her, huh?"

"Why do you think someone would want to murder her?"

He crunched some ice and seemed to be considering my question. "I'm sorry she's gone. She was in charge of my trust, you know." He rolled his eyes. "Can you believe the old codger, my grandfather, had my inheritance held in trust until I'm thirty? Thirty! Hell, I might as well be ninety. All those years, wasted."

"Imagine that." I steered him back on track. "What does Cecile's murder have to do with your trust?"

"Well, she was administrator, you see." He leaned an elbow on the bar and attempted to rest his head on his upturned palm but somehow missed and nearly smashed his chin onto the bar. He recovered admirably and went on talking as if nothing had happened. He was three sheets gone already. *I better hurry and get what I need out of him.* "But it was working out pretty sweet for me. I had the old biddy wrapped around my pinky." He wiggled said digit at me. "When I needed money, she was Johnny-on-the-spot with the checkbook." He looked down the bar and lifted his hand to signal the bartender. I reached over and lowered his hand.

"But nobody else seemed to like her much, except Terrence the Caterpillar Man." He giggled. "The Society of the Lepidop-whatsit Alien Caterpillar, yada yada yada. Baby, did he have her snowed. Ya gotta hand it to him."

"Him?"

"You know, Terrence. That worm—get it, worm?—was soaking the old girl for every nickel he could get out of her."

"He was?"

His lids were getting droopy. I hoped he didn't nod off to sleep while I was trying to interview him. "Mmm, he thought she was going to boogie down the aisle with him, and he'd be Mr. Moneybags. Sucker."

"She wasn't going to marry him?"

"Hell no. She found out his fuzzy little caterpillars weren't exactly endangered after all. In some places they're so hardy, they're trying to get rid of them. She was going to break it off with him and find herself a new squeeze to keep her warm at night. Maybe one who didn't take money from her under false pretenses."

"Oh." Sounded like excellent motive to me—about to lose your payday and murdering your intended before she could cut the purse strings and change her will. People kill for less. At least that's what they say on TV.

And speaking of money… "Billy, were you aware your grandmother—"

"Cecile was my stepgrandmother. You know step—like Cinderella? Snow White? Only she didn't make me scrub floors or try to poison me with apples." He seemed to realize what he'd said and sat pensively while the moment passed.

"Did you know she had a hundred thousand dollars in cash with her?"

"I do now," he said. "But she didn't tell me about it, if that's what you want to know. I heard it from that swamp cop." He must have liked the sound of that. He said it a few times. "Swamp cop. Swamp cop. He said she had it, and someone took it." He shrugged. "That's all I know. She had it. I'd like to have it, but someone else beat me to it."

Billy leaned closer, squinting at me. He nearly fell off his barstool. "So whatcha think 'bout that, sugar britches?" He was slurring now.

Sugar britches. That was a new one. For some reason, an image of Cap'n Jack popped into my head. Now that was some sugar britches, all right.

"What I think is," I said, "we need to get you upstairs to bed."

"Hallelujah!" He slid off the stool. I caught him under the arms, but he still draped all over me like an old quilt.

The bartender, a pretty girl I didn't remember meeting before this, walked over and shoved her princess hat back off her forehead. "You need me to call someone?"

I nodded. "Mr. Whitlock's had a little more than he can handle."

"No, no." He looked up at me through unfocused eyes. "I can handle it." He lifted his right hand and put it square on top of my boob. "See?"

* * *

Lurch picked up Billy like he was a six-year-old and put him over his shoulder. He grumbled all the way up the stairs, down the hall, and into the room. Billy hummed the theme song from the *Addams Family*, snapping his fingers at the appropriate moment.

Before Lurch deposited him on top of his bed, he pulled out his cell phone and snapped off a selfie of himself and Billy Whitlock's butt.

Just as Lurch shut the door to Billy's room, Penelope Devere, Cecile Elway's psychic consultant, came up the hall.

Lurch grumbled and reached for his cell phone. I laid my hand on his arm, which brought another grumble as he lumbered off to the stairs.

"Is there something going on with William Whitlock?" she asked.

"Billy? Not really, Ms. Devere," I said. "He sort of over-imbibed on hurricanes."

"Oh, my lands, that young man," she exclaimed. "And, by the way, if you don't call me Penny, I won't know who you're talking to."

"Do you mind if I walk with you?"

She shrugged. "Suit yourself. I'm heading downstairs to the Hidden Passage Spa. I hear it isn't easy to find. Maybe you can show me?"

Penny Devere was about my height, five foot two or three, and slightly stout. If I had to guess her age, I would have said midfifties. It didn't appear she'd lived a privileged life—her face sagged at the jowls and her neck reminded me of a turkey. If

I had to choose a color for Penny, it would be khaki. Her hair was a nondescript brown, and she wore it pulled back away from her face caught in the back with a wide barrette. The tone of her skin was a little on the sallow side, and her eyes were a light hazel. She wore brown plastic-framed eyeglasses. While she wasn't ugly, she wasn't attractive either—the sort of person you could pass by every day for a year, yet still not have noticed her enough to be able to describe her accurately.

"Such a shame about Mrs. Elway. I'm sorry for your loss." It was that lame statement everyone makes when they have no other words to express their regret your life has been turned upside down. But Penny didn't seem to notice the triteness of it.

"Thank you," she said. "A loss is exactly what it was. Cecile was like a sister to me."

Of course. So far, it seemed like Cecile Elway was all things to all people. Everyone loved her, or at least said they did. "You know, the police have determined she was murdered. Poisoned."

"Right," she said.

"Oh, you knew? Who told you?"

"Well, my dear," she said patiently, "I *am* psychic."

And I *am* the Queen of England. "So, do you also know who killed her?"

Again, the sigh and condescending attitude. "The cosmos doesn't work that way, but I'm fairly certain the hand of death struck her from beyond the grave."

Okay. "You think she was murdered by the ghost of Theodore Elway?"

She shrugged. "Well, he did order the clams."

"I thought Cecile asked for the clams."

"In essence, I suppose she did. In fact, if you want to get all technical about it, I suppose you could say I ordered the clams."

"You?"

She nodded. "The spirit of Theodore came to me in a dream. He said his soul was restless, and he needed Cecile to help him find peace, that I was to bring Cecile here for a séance with the Great Fabrizio. He told me he had to communicate directly with her, that to prove her good intentions and love for him, during the séance she should provide a dozen clams on the half shell." She was thoughtful. "But no wonder he killed her. The ignorant fool forgot the hot sauce."

I said, "Spirits are known to get riled up pretty easy."

She looked sideways at me. It was hard to tell if she suspected I was putting her on.

"Of course, if you ask Rosalyn..."

Rosalyn—Theodore's daughter, Cecile's stepdaughter.

"...the ghost of Theodore Elway had better motive than forgotten hot sauce for offing his widow."

"And that would be...?"

"Revenge." So matter-of-fact. "Rosalyn has always believed Cecile Elway in essence murdered Theodore."

Whoa. Hold your horses. "Rosalyn Elway Whitlock believes her stepmother murdered him?"

"Her words, not mine. She never said murdered. She said 'caused.' 'She caused my father's death.'"

"Wow," I said. "I had no idea. It doesn't sound as if Cecile Elway was all that popular after all."

"Well, I wouldn't say that." The look on her face was smug. "She always had old Terrence, you know, of the Society of the..."

"Lopsey-dopsey-whatever Alien Caterpillars?"

She nodded, smiling.

"But I heard she was about to cut him loose."

She looked a bit surprised. "Really? Who told you that?"

"Billy."

"Oh, well, he never liked Terrence. Always felt threatened by him. Worried that Cecile's marrying Terrence would somehow threaten his inheritance. He was wrong of course. His trust is airtight. Theodore—Mr. Elway—saw to that. It figures Billy would try to put Terrence in a bad light. He didn't like him."

"What about you," I asked. "Did you like him?"

"Well, why not? I figure live and let live. Right? I say, 'Attaboy, Terrence. You go get her.'"

Her cell phone went off. It was Gordon Lightfoot "If You Could Read My Mind." She snatched it from her purse and silently read what was on the screen then she squealed like a twelve-year-old at a Justin Bieber concert. "Oh, joy, it's happened. It's happened." She twirled in a circle. "I'm officially the president of the International Paranormal Society." She was beaming. "I've waited a long time, you know."

Right, and such an honor it is, too.

We stopped in the hallway just down from Dragons and Deities. To the casual observer, it appeared to be nothing more than the hallway of an old-fashioned plantation house. No real purpose. Nothing sinister or hidden. But when you looked more closely, you could see that the wainscot panels were about seven feet high and about three and a half feet wide. Just the size of a doorway. And when someone just happened to reach up and pull on one of the light sconces, the middle panel would groan and moan and slowly swing open to reveal the Hidden Passage Salon and Spa.

"If you don't know who murdered Cecile, do you know who took the money she had hidden in her room?"

"The money she brought down as incentive for a successful séance?" She nodded. "I do. Don't you?"

I shook my head, waiting. My heartbeat kicked up a notch.

"It was that Fabrizio fellow, wasn't it? That's what the police told me."

I was crushed. "That's what the sheriff's office thinks. Yes. That Fabrizio stole it."

"But you don't?" She took off her glasses and began to chew on one of the tips. "Who do you think took it?"

I shrugged. "Only part of it was found in Fabrizio's room. Just enough to make him look suspicious. Whoever has the rest of it might just be the same person who killed your friend. But I don't know who that is. I was hoping you could tell me. You're the psychic."

Her smile was wry. "Like I said before, the cosmos doesn't work that way. If they did, I'd play the five-hundred-dollar tables in Atlantic City, have a heavy-duty stock portfolio, and have won the lottery five or six times already." She looked at her watch. "I need to get to the spa now, or I'll miss my appointment. I thought you were going to walk me there."

"I did," I said and pulled the sconce just above my head.

Penny squealed in delight as the panel slid open. "Oh, my. Isn't that just too much? You know, I forgot all about these. When we took a tour of The Mansion our first day, the guide showed us several of these creepy passages." She thanked me and went inside.

The panel closed behind her, squeaking and creaking the way it was designed to by Harry Villars's whacked-out architect, who was like a kid in a candy store when Harry asked him to turn his plantation home into a "haunted mansion."

CHAPTER ELEVEN

Deputy Quincy Boudreaux showed up at the hotel sometime after 7:30 p.m. Thursday night. It was an official visit complete with a squad car and wingman—make that wingwoman, Sergeant Mackelroy.

I was on my way to "my room" from the main kitchen where I'd had dinner, coffee, and conversation with the fabulous Valentine Cantrell, who'd whipped up some awesome shrimp creole, and per Jack's pre-approval, had made enough for the entire staff on duty to have a serving. My last appointment for the day hadn't left my parlor until after six thirty, so I was later than most of the rest of the staff to head down to the kitchen. Valentine hadn't eaten yet either, so she filled a bowl and joined me, and we sat together and commiserated over how to help Fabrizio out of this mess.

Who should I run into but Cap'n Jack, looking extremely fine in snug, straight-leg grey slacks and a French blue shirt with the collar unbuttoned and sleeves pushed up on his forearms. A silver-and-blue-striped tie hung loosely knotted around his neck, lending the impression he'd been interrupted in the middle of getting dressed. That thought alone made me warm in places a Southern lady doesn't mention.

"Nice to see you, Melanie." His voice was low, intimate, barely audible over "Skylark" from the piano bar in the main salon.

I swallowed the *Cap'n* and just said, "Jack."

One corner of his mouth turned up. His eyes moved over me top to bottom and back up, seeming to stop on my mouth. It made me catch my breath. Gosh, I wished he wasn't my boss, but if he weren't my boss, I never would have even met him.

"On your way to your room?" The way he said *room* sounded more like *bed* to me, but that was probably just the frame of mind I was in.

I nodded. "Thinking about making it an early night."

Something flickered in his eyes, and it occurred to me the idea of a bed in my hotel room hadn't gotten completely by him either. "Well, good night then."

That was when Quincy and said wingwoman walked up and handed Jack a folded document. "Mr. Stockton?"

Jack turned. "Just Jack's fine."

Quincy grinned. Jack hadn't yet learned not to give a Cajun a straight line like that. "Okay. Just Jack, this is a duly processed search warrant covering the public areas of The Mansion for the purpose of determining the source of poison used in the homicide of Cecile Elway on Sunday last."

Jack's face paled. "Why would you…?"

"The tox screen results indicate she was done in with a grade of poison used in several commercial products that might be used in the maintenance of a property such as this one." He smiled, showing even, pearly whites.

I was impressed. That was way more words than had ever come out of Quincy's mouth at one time. And he was still on a roll.

"I'd like to start where your housekeeping staff stores their supplies, also the maintenance shed. Once I determine the source of the toxins, I'll be in the mood to interview a few people who have access." He turned that brilliant smile on Jack, whose business demeanor was back in place.

"I understand," Jack said. "Please, Deputy, if you need anything, let me know. I'll put out the word my staff should cooperate with you any way they can."

Quincy nodded. "If you'll just point Sergeant Mackelroy in the direction of the housekeeping supply stores, I'll head on over to the maintenance building."

I jumped at the chance to talk to him. "This way, Quincy. I'll take you."

* * *

As we neared the boat dock and old boathouse, Quincy's radio hissed and Sergeant Mackelroy's voice announced, "Didn't find nothing in housekeeping, Boudreaux."

So none of the chemicals they were looking for had been used in any of the cleaning supplies. Next up was the boathouse.

As we neared the pond, we met Odeo, the groundskeeper, coming our way.

He touched the bill of his cap, nodded, and smiled his big, toothy grin. "Evening, y'all."

Before I could reply, Quincy stopped him. "Just the man I been looking for. You wouldn't mind giving me a run-through of what you keep on the grounds for weed control, bugs, stuff like that."

Odeo frowned but said, "Sure, boss, you da law. Whatever you want, I want. Just follow me." He stepped back and motioned for me to go ahead of him. "Miss Melanie."

I led the two men to the boathouse, where Odeo used his key to unlock the door.

* * *

Once we were inside, Quincy asked Odeo to show him all kinds of weird things: paint thinner, weed spray, ant and roach killer, rat poison, all manner of lovely things.

He seemed to have the most interest in a five-gallon bucket of insecticide granules. Odeo set it up on a workbench, and Quincy pulled a sheet of paper from his shirt pocket.

When he looked at me, he said, "Tox results," and showed me the paper. "This is what we're after, Mel," he said. "This here." He pointed at it, and I instantly saw why he didn't try to pronounce it. The word was about a foot and a half long, with bunches of consonants strung together and an amazing number of *x*'s, *y*'s, and *z*'s to be in one word.

"And this here looks like a winner." He shone his penlight on the label wrapped around the bucket, specifically on the ingredients. And although I wouldn't have thought it possible, that same long word was reproduced there. "Looks like maybe we found the source of the dressing our killer used on dem clams." He laughed.

I personally didn't see the humor in it.

Odeo pried off the lid and handed a pair of garden gloves to Quincy, who slipped them on and dipped his hand inside the bucket. He came up with a fistful of small white granules. The odor from the bucket was strong enough to make my eyes and nose sting. I stood back some. "Is that it?" I asked. "Is that what killed her?"

Quincy tipped his head and did a little shuffle, extending his hand to display the granules. "If it looks like a duck and walks like a duck..."

"...and smells like a duck," I added, wrinkling my nose.

"And don't forget quacks like a duck..." Odeo added.

Quincy and I looked at him. "Quacks?" we said together.

Odeo shrugged. "I just thought...never y'all mind."

Quincy got back to it. "So now I'm thinking what we need to do is figure out when our good man Fabrizio had a chance to make his way out to this here shed and dip into the bucket for a small sample to spice up dem clams special for Missus Elway."

My hackles rose. "Fabrizio? Are you still singing that old song? Fabrizio didn't—couldn't kill Mrs. Elway. Why are you stuck in that rut? Look somewhere else for a killer, why don't you?"

He narrowed his eyes. "You forgetting your pal had the opportunity? You forgetting he had the motive? And are you forgetting he had the money?"

I threw up my hands. "He was framed."

"Show me evidence he was framed, and I'll sing you a new tune, Mel." Not only was he singing the same song, he kept repeating the chorus. "I'm looking for a killer, Mel. A cold-blooded sort of person who planned it all out and went through with it. This ain't no crime of passion. It's hard-core, premeditated murder, and whether you want to admit it or not, so far everything points to Fabrizio Banini. Like I said, if it looks like a duck..."

"Quack, quack," Odeo said.

I burst into tears and ran out.

Behind me, Odeo said, "What d'ya think she's got against ducks, anyway?"

CHAPTER TWELVE

———

I was so frustrated, I hardly slept at all that night. Quincy was like a mean li'l ol' bulldog with a big ol' bone, and he wasn't about to let it go. It was almost like he had it in for Fabrizio. I knew Fabrizio didn't take that money, and he certainly hadn't murdered Cecile Elway. That just didn't make any sense at all, but it was beginning to look like it was f'sure up to me to prove it.

I woke up extra early Friday morning to clear skies and a bright sun. Both bode well for Harry and Jack's first annual Mansion at Mystic Isle Crawfish Boil to be held that night.

I had two tats lined up for the morning and had been recruited to help with arrangements for the Crawfish Boil later, which left me a couple of hours free in the middle of the day to find and interview the next person on my list. A sense of urgency moved me forward. I had a very bad feeling if I couldn't get to the bottom of this mystery sooner than later, Fabrizio would pay, and the check he'd have to write would be huge.

The next person I wanted to speak with was Rosalyn, Theodore Elway's daughter and Cecile's stepdaughter, who, according to Penny the Psychic, had a steaming hatred brewing to a boil for her recently deceased stepmother.

It took me a good while to find Rosalyn Elway Whitlock. But finally there she was, playing solitaire with a deck of house cards in the deepest, darkest corner of the small alcove, just off the Presto-Change-o Room. While the bar and food service areas were buzzing with late lunchers, the game room was all but abandoned. Stella by Starlight, the resort's astrologer, was at one of the tables casting a chart. Across from her, a stern-looking woman sat impatiently tapping her fingernails on the tabletop. The customer's white hair was cut in a precise, Prince Valiant pageboy. Everything about her was exact and contained, from her buttoned-up Oxford-style shirt to her sensible, lace-up walking shoes. Virgo, if I ever saw one. As I walked past their table, Stella, still graceful and lovely at seventy-two, looked up and smiled, pushing errant locks of curly, silver hair from her face.

They were the only two people in the room except Rosalyn. She looked down at the cards, her eyes flitting from one stack to the next and back as she rubbed the bridge of her nose and shook her head, clenching then unclenching her fists. I honestly felt sorry for her. The poor thing was wound up tighter than her permed hair. If you opened the dictionary to *uptight*, I was pretty sure Rosalyn's picture would be there. Cancer, definitely a July baby.

I stopped by her table. When she looked up, I fully expected her to shatter into a thousand pieces—she appeared to be that stressed.

"Yes?" she said. "What is it?"

I sighed and looked at her cards. "You can move that four of hearts off." I pointed.

She looked back up at me. "You're the young woman who was at the séance."

I nodded. "I don't suppose you'd have time to talk to me?"

She snorted. It was odd and unattractive in such a prim-and-proper person. "Time? I'm not exactly in high demand here." She laid the cards on the table and lifted her hand toward the chair across from her. "What can I do for you?"

"I was wondering about your relationship to your stepmother. Did the two of you, er, get along all right?"

"Get along? I supposed that depends on your definition of the term." She folded her hands in front of her. "My father never really got over my mother's passing. Cecile looked a good deal like her, you know. He was smitten from the first time he saw her." Her smile was rueful. "He never had a chance, really."

I didn't speak, thinking it might slow her down or stop her.

She took a deep breath and began to draw circles on the tabletop with her index finger. "He couldn't deny her anything, and therein lay the problem. Cecile came from trashy people who somehow managed to weasel their way into the better social circles. She liked to pretend she wasn't trash, but she couldn't fool me. She was going through the family fortune like there was an endless supply. Father was worried. He confided in me he planned to have a talk with her. I could tell it weighed on him. And then she took up with that charlatan caterpillar person." She leaned forward onto her elbows and lowered her voice. "She swore they weren't sleeping together before my father passed, but well, you know."

"So, you feel like your daddy passed away before his time because she broke his heart?"

She pressed her lips together, hard, bringing out little vertical lines over her upper lip—the ones women get from pursing their lips in disapproval all the time. She nodded, just once, decisively. "Cecile was *not* a woman of substance."

I sat back in my chair and just looked at her. Even in the low lighting, the hate that shone in her eyes was pretty scary.

"She acted as if our money was her money, the witch."

"Oh," I said. "Billy sort of gave me the impression Cecile was pretty generous in doling out funds."

"Generous?" She laughed, but it sounded more like a bark. "Maybe to Billy. You know all that boy has to do is smile, and women just fall down at his feet. Even Cecile."

"So she was more tightfisted when it came to you?"

Again, that curt bob of her head. "And it wasn't even her money. I don't know what Father was thinking leaving that squanderer in control of his estate." She huffed, stood, and swept some of the cards off the table. I fully expected smoke to start pouring out her ears. "It was humiliating to have to crawl on my hands and knees and grovel just to get what little I needed to maintain my lifestyle." She threw her hands in the air. "I mean, my God, you'd have thought I was the one tossing money around like it was confetti, not her. I mean, caterpillars? Really?"

Made sense to me. What also made sense was how someone who held so much resentment toward another person might be motivated to put insecticide in her séance snacks.

She'd begun to pace back and forth by the table. Pretty stirred up. More passion than I would have given her credit for. "I confronted her with it, you know. Just hours before the séance. 'Cecile,' I said. 'You have no right to make such a grant to that man and his ugly little creatures.'"

"Terrence? You mean Terrence, right?"

She didn't act as if she'd heard me. "And when she laughed and suggested I was only angry because she had a man in her bed and I didn't—I slapped her. I did. Right across the face. So hard she stumbled and nearly fell. Do you blame me?"

Couldn't say as I did, if it was even true. I couldn't picture Rosalyn lifting a hand to anyone. But then, insinuating someone's a dried up old hag no man would ever even look at is enough to get any woman riled—even mousey Rosalyn.

"Rosalyn?"

She stopped and looked down at me.

"Were you aware your stepmother came here with a large amount of cash?"

"We all were, after she was killed, that is. Deputy Boudreaux said something about a huge sum of cash being missing."

"And you didn't know about it before then?"

She shook her head. "No." Some of the steam seemed to have left her, and she began to look around, a little at a loss. "Maybe I should—"

"One more thing," I said. "Penny told me you believe Cecile might have died by...otherworldly means."

She looked amused. "Penny said that?"

I nodded.

"Penny the Psychic?"

I shrugged, feeling foolish. Who in their right mind would actually believe the ghost of her deceased father would reach out from beyond the grave and toss a little insecticide into a dozen clams on the half shell?

"She's right. I do think that."

Okay then. Guess that answered that.

She narrowed her eyes—I could hardly wait to hear what she had to say next. "And that's not all. I believe the ghost of my wicked, wicked step-mother has come back to haunt me."

"You do?"

Her eyes got this troubled, faraway look in them. "I hear her at night, taunting me, berating me, just the way she used to. Once when I woke up, I thought I even saw her in the corner of my room. That's why I came out here to sit. Whenever I'm in that room, I can't help but feel as if someone's watching me. It's creepy."

I thought of the portrait of Alphonse Villars with the shifty eyes that was still sitting in the closet of my room.

Creepy? She was right. It was. And it even made me wonder if Theodore and Cecile Elway were roaming the halls of The Mansion at Mystic Isle.

* * *

The grounds behind The Mansion sloped up to the edge of the property, beyond which lay a wooded area and more swampland.

Odeo and his staff kept the lawn lush and green year round. The setup for the Crawfish Boil had been going on for three days. There were two outdoor kitchens with a multitude of boiling pots on either side of the tables and chairs, and a bandstand in between. The contingency in case of rain was to set up tents closer in to the main building, but the weatherman had promised clear skies until tomorrow, so it looked like the guests would be peeling their crawfish and shoveling in corn on the cob, hush puppies, and boiled potatoes under a starry sky.

Valentine's cousin Ernest had rounded up a couple of his buddies, and they all brought in their two-day catch, which weighed in upward of seven hundred pounds of squirming crawfish, all climbing over each other in a futile attempt to make a break for it before they got their butts tossed in the boil seasoned with Valentine's spicy crawfish boil seasoning.

Valentine would take command of one of the outdoor kitchens, her sous chef the other.

At seven that night the C'est la Vie Boys would show up and swing us all into some lively *fais-do-do* Zydeco music. It promised to be a huge success. I just wished Fabrizio could be here with Mr. Villars to share the fun.

*   *   *

Cat and I were just sitting down to dig in when I looked up and saw Cap'n Jack wandering around looking a little lost.

I got up, went to him, and hooked him by the arm. "Come and sit with us."

He hesitated. "I should probably sit with some of the guests."

"Oh, no, *cher*," I teased, doing my best Quincy Boudreaux imitation. "Dem Yankees, dey won't be teaching you how to eat crawdaddies."

Jack smiled, his eyes glimmering. "It drives me crazy when you speak French," he said, catching me by surprise as he fell in step with me. "Guess I better come with you for a proper lesson."

We sat him down, put a bib on him, and signaled a waiter, who brought three trays loaded up with crawfish, potatoes, corn, and hush puppies.

He picked up one of the little red suckers, twisting it and turning it around to have a really good look. "Looks like a puny lobster," he said.

I nodded agreement, picked up a nice, fat juicy one, and elbowed him. "And this is how it goes. First you pull the tail straight then push it in to break loose the meat." I did it. "Pull it back out all the way, and there you go." I popped it in my mouth and sucked off the meat.

He had watched me closely then picked one up and looked at it dubiously before repeating what I'd done. He chewed, swallowed, then turned and smiled. "Oh. My. God. These rock." He wiped his mouth and picked up another.

And so it went. He must have gone through about thirty or so of Valentine's spicy crawfish. He even sampled all the dips on the lazy Susan in the middle of the table—bar-b-que, sriracha, white vinegar, lemon, seasoned melted butter. And he said he liked them all.

He drank beer and ate corn on the cob like a kid, row after row. If he were a woman, you'd have said he let his hair down. He talked and laughed and told me Big Apple stories. And I loved it. Every minute.

After a bit, he turned and looked at me, laying his hand on top of mine. I jerked at the contact. It was like a buzz of current ran between us. "Will you walk with me?" he asked.

Hell, yeah.

I stood, and he sort of steered me away from the crowd. The music faded into the background. We stopped under a big old weeping willow. He used his hand to brush off one of the elaborate wrought iron benches then motioned me to sit.

He sat beside me.

"Melanie," he began then stopped. "I don't really know where to begin."

This didn't sound like the usual shoptalk. I held my breath.

"I've been here a couple of months now. Things are going pretty well. I'd be lying if I said I wasn't worried at first. That situation in New York had me plenty scared I'd never work in the industry again. But Mr. Villars, Harry, came to my rescue. I guess you could say he pulled me out of the swamp and set me on solid ground."

He stopped again and took hold of my hand. I could barely breathe. I knew what he was going to say, something about how much he liked me but how he didn't dare risk his job by getting involved. It made me sad.

"Harry sat down with me earlier to go over a few of the details for tonight's party." He waved his free hand back in the direction of the shindig, which was going full blast now. "I took a chance and spoke to him about…us. You and me. And how I was feeling about you, about wanting to get to know you better. We talked about how if the boss took advantage of his position with female staff members, it could be harassment, and how I didn't want to be inappropriate with an employee. He said…"

Ohmigod. Here it came. He was going to break my heart into a million pieces.

He slid into a fair imitation of Harry, although it sounded more like a Tennessee drawl than New Orleans-style English. "'You know, Jack, I took a shine to you the minute we met. And part of the reason I hired you, besides your fabulous resume and manly good looks, is that you aren't Fabrizio's type. Harassment? Inappropriate? Why, Jack, you don't have an inappropriate bone in your body, son. And Miss Hamilton, why I can tell she's a real Southern lady. I'd be honored to have a part in bringing you two lovely people together.'"

I blinked, trying awfully hard to figure out what the man had just told me.

"So." He stood and pulled me to him, body to body. He leaned down, his breath warm against my ear. "What do you say, Miss Hamilton? Want to be my girl?"

I looked up into his eyes, like dark pools with just a glimmer of moonlight in them. "Why, Mr. Stockton, are you courting me?"

"You bet your grits I am."

He leaned down, his lips so close to mine a small movement would cause our mouths to collide in what I knew would be a crash of cymbals and thunder of tympani.

A small smile curved his lips, like he knew a secret. I caught my breath as he inched closer then jerked back at—

"Ah, so here y'all are."

Deputy Quincy Boudreaux strolled up. If I had a gun, I'd have shot him dead.

"Hope I didn't interrupt nothin'."

Jack cleared his throat. "What can we do for you, Deputy?"

Quincy looked at me and shook his head. "I figured you'd want to hear the bad news right away, *chère*."

"Why would you think that, Q? Nobody in his right mind wants to hear bad news, ever." I glared at him.

"We got a warrant to search Fabrizio's room at Mr. Villars's residence."

Oh, man, he was right. If he thought this was bad news, it was probably horrible.

"We found these in your friend's closet." He held up a big clear plastic bag that contained a pair of work boots. "Mr. Villars confirmed they belong to Fabrizio. He uses them for puttering around in the garden behind the little house. The treads of the soles are imbedded up with what we're pretty sure is that toxic insecticide we found in the old boathouse. You know what this means."

I didn't have to say anything. He could probably tell by the look on my face I knew what insecticide on the boots meant, but he said it anyway.

"We'll be charging Fabrizio Banini with the murder of Cecile Elway."

CHAPTER THIRTEEN

Talk about a mood killer.

Poor Fabrizio. I was beside myself, and when Jack and I arrived back at the table, it must have been obvious to everyone around me.

"What's wrong?"

"What happened?"

"Oh, my goodness, Mel, you look like you've seen a…"

I stood and excused myself and headed back to the main building, Jack right beside me, holding my hand. He hadn't said a word yet, but I didn't really expect or want him to.

My head spun with the horrible, terrible news of what was about to happen to dear, sweet, never ever hurt a fly Fabrizio.

Coming across the lawn, we met Terrence Montague moving at a brisk clip. He seemed excited, animated. "Have you heard?"

I didn't answer, too upset to worry about him or his worms.

"They've made an arrest. It was the medium. The Great Fabrizio."

"No." But it was a whisper so soft, I barely heard it myself.

"Insecticide. They said it was all over his boots. Huh. You know that particular brand is highly toxic. It would have been like drinking Drano."

I stared at him. "Drano? How do you know so much—"

He spoke right over me. "About bug killer? Really, Miss Hamilton? Have you forgotten who I am, what species I champion? That's like asking someone who's allergic to peanuts what he knows about peanut butter. Well, sort of."

Oh. Right. He was the bug man.

"And what I know is that specific commercial insecticide is reserved for some particularly nasty infestations." He glanced at Jack. "Frankly, I'm surprised they allow you to keep it around here, the bayou environment being so delicate and all."

Jack said, "It was fire ants. They were taking over. We had to get a special permit to use the insecticide just once to get rid of them. They're very particular about protecting the ecosystem down here."

"At least it wasn't caterpillars," Terrence said.

I could only stare at him openmouthed. Here was someone who knew all about the nasty stuff that had killed Mrs. Elway. I had no doubt if you asked Fabrizio about how to kill insects, he'd suggest a baseball bat. Yet the problem was the toxic substance was all over Fabrizio's boots, not Terrence's.

Upon entering the main lobby, a tragic sight met our eyes—the usually whimsical and dapper figure of Harry Villars crumpled on the floor, his back up against the granite-topped check-in counter, crying as if his heart had been torn from him and shredded.

Inappropriate or not, I dropped to my knees and wrapped my arms around him. He turned into me, soaking the shoulder of my dress with his tears.

"Shush now, Mr. Villars. It'll be okay. We're not going to let anything happen to him."

"He...he...he..." He hiccupped. "They...they...they..."

I looked up at Jack, who paced back and forth a few feet away. "Jack?"

He stopped pacing and helped Harry to his feet, offering him a clean handkerchief after Harry blew his nose loudly on his own monogrammed hanky.

Harry nodded his appreciation, one hand still clutching mine. He turned watery eyes to me. "Miss Hamilton, Mr. Stockton, I must apologize for losing control of myself in that manner. The weight of those awful charges they're about to bring against Fabrizio just broke my heart right in two."

I patted his hand. "Try not to worry, Mr. Villars. I have no intention of letting the real killer get away. I've begun my own investigation."

Harry blinked several times. "You have?"

I nodded.

"With what results? Are there any leads? Any hope to exonerate the Great Fabrizio?"

I took a breath and looked at Jack. Poor Mr. Villars was so upset, so fragile at that moment, I couldn't bear having to tell him that while I'd gathered quite a bit of information, none of it seemed to amount to anything. Not yet, anyway.

That was when Jack's voice, soft, caring, Yankee or not, managed the tone I couldn't. "Miss Hamilton has learned a great deal, Harry. Unless I miss my guess, she's getting closer to identifying the real killer all the time. It shouldn't take much more to tie things up and take her findings to the sheriff, and with your approval, I'll help her."

Harry drew himself up, tugged on his jacket lapels and cuffs, bent to retrieve his white straw skimmer off the floor, and nodded to Jack. "By all means, Mr. Stockton. Any assistance you lend to the release of our friend, employee, and most beloved Fabrizio will put me forever in your debt."

"No, Mr. Villars," Jack said, "it won't. Not at all. Now that the charges are being made, I'm compelled to get involved and see what can be done. It's the right thing to do."

Cap'n Jack. My hero. My eyes stung with tears of appreciation, mingling with tears of worry over dear Fabrizio.

"Thank you, Jack," Harry said. "I best be getting back to *la petite maison* and call my lawyer. He's getting on in years, and these days he's in bed asleep by eight o'clock. He won't be happy to get the call, but he's been the family counselor for decades. He'll do what needs to be done."

Harry Villars shook Jack's hand, laid his other hand on my shoulder, and bobbed his head in a gesture of gratitude and acknowledgement.

People were beginning to filter in every few minutes from the back entrances. The *fais-do-do* must have been winding down. Even the band seemed to have kicked into a dreamier playlist. Strains of Sam Cooke's "A Change Is Gonna Come" floated in and out as the doors opened and closed.

"Where do we go from here, Mel?" Jack asked, his voice still soft and considerate.

I looked up at him, earnest, compassionate, and so studly. The double entendre didn't get by me. He'd been about to make a move before Quincy showed up, and I'd been ready and waiting for him to do it.

Whenever a new "suitor," as Mama used to call them, would stroll into her life, she'd always be happy. "Timing is everything, Mellie," she'd say. And when they made their exit, she'd always be just as philosophical and utter those same words, "Timing is everything, Mellie."

Her timing to this day wasn't worth a darn. I hoped that *osculum interruptus*, as Caesar would say, out under the willow tree wasn't a sign crappy timing runs in the family.

But the good-timing theory definitely applied to more than romance. It probably had to do with turning over stones and finding a snake. If I was going to help Fabrizio, I needed to get busy flipping over those rocks and seeing just what lay beneath.

"I believe I'll try to get to sleep early," I said. "I have a feeling tomorrow is going to be a real doozy of a day."

He walked me to my room at the far end of the auxiliary wing. Neither of us said a word until we stopped at my door. It was an awkward moment, at least for me.

Jack didn't seem to be uncomfortable in the least. "If you aren't too tired, I could come in."

He caught me by surprise. "Oh," I said. "What for?"

From the look on his face, I caught him by surprise too. He arched one gorgeous brow, "Gee, I dunno," he said, sarcasm heavy in his tone, "a bedtime story?"

My face warmed, and I knew I was turning pink under his steady gaze. But now wasn't the time to be a shrinking violet. I took him by the hand and led him into my lair.

The standard double room in the auxiliary wing at The Mansion on Mystic Isle wasn't a suite at the Ritz, but for a hotel room there was more character than usual—even those that hadn't been updated yet to the haunted mansion mode, like mine. Two double beds with the resort's standard pewter-tone metal headboards in the French style. The nightstands, dresser, and sitting area were furnished in Louis XIV replicas—some of the rooms had off-white pieces, but the furniture in this one was a soft rose. Draperies and wallpaper brought to mind a gentler, antebellum era. The only jarring note was the flat-screen on the wall opposite the beds.

Jack tucked his hand in his jeans pockets and sauntered over to one of the beds. He sat, bounced a couple of times (which made me giggle), and then patted the empty spot beside him.

I sat down and turned to mush when he circled his arms around me.

It was what I'd been thinking about, dreaming about for two and a half months, ever since the first day Jack walked into the resort lobby to take over after the last in a long string of failed managers. Harry Villars and his investors, his four cousins who won *Family Feud* and invested their winnings in the resort by paying off the back taxes, had brought in men and women— one or two of which whose gender was questionable—to try and pull the resort (kicking and screaming) into a profitable state. Giselle Martine, the resort's general manager just before Jack, had only lasted six weeks before her high-handed ways sent her packing. She came from a South Carolina bed-and-breakfast and was more interested in redecorating the place and trying out new scone recipes than she was in bringing in new business, handling the day-to-day operations, and pleasing the guests.

Jack Stockton arrived on the scene in a three-piece suit with all that New York state-of-mind baggage. But he was a happy medium between the previously retired uninspired stiffs and Giselle's loosey-goosey style. In the ten weeks he'd been there, business had picked up, employees were content, and the hotel was humming along like a Delta Queen riverboat heading downstream.

Oh, and I believe I've already mentioned, he was the tastiest piece of eye candy ever.

He stretched out to the nightstand and flipped on the radio. Sarah Vaughn was "Misty," and so was I.

Something about being there with Jack filled me with emotion.

As he straightened up, cupped my chin in his hand, and leaned in to kiss me, I began to cry.

Dammit.

He didn't quite know what to do, and neither did I.

"Oh," he said. "Is it me? Is it something I did? I thought you wanted—"

"I do," I said. "It's not you. It's just..."

His eyes softened. "Fabrizio," he said. "I understand." He got off the bed and walked to the dresser, snagged a couple of Kleenex, and handed them to me.

I blew my nose. Romantic, right?

He sat back down. "Tell me what you've learned so far."

"You're really going to help me?" I said. "Us? You're really going to help us?"

"Of course. Why wouldn't I?"

I wanted to throw my arms around his neck and plant one on him. Our eyes met and held. It was one of those moments when time nearly stood still, and if it had been a scene from a movie, our lips would have met, an orchestra would have played, and sparks would have flown. But I just didn't feel like it was the right time and maybe not even the right place for our first kiss. I pulled back, and the moment passed. Regret flashed in his eyes, but only briefly.

"I'm just so glad you're going to help us, and it just confirms what I've always thought about you," I said.

His eyebrows shot up. "Which is...?"

"You're a really nice man, Cap'n Jack. And I think I just might be crazy about you."

He smiled and took hold of my hand, squeezing softly. "Aye, wench." It was a fair impression of Long John Silver. "If it's crazy yer wantin', I might be just what yer lookin' for."

We raided the minibar and talked a while about what came from the interviews with Terrence the Caterpillar Man, Billy the grandson, Rosalyn the stepdaughter, and Penny the Psychic.

I told him about Terrence's kept-man status and how he was about to lose his meal ticket because Cecile found out his caterpillar conservancy was a fake. I told him that after Billy's grandfather died, Cecile was named administrator of Billy

Whitlock's trust-fund money until his thirtieth birthday, and the boy was impatient to get his hands on it, and that Rosalyn Elway Whitlock had absolutely no use for the money-grubbing woman who broke her father's heart, hastened his death, and was going through the family fortune like it was hot butter. Two of them, Penny and Terrence, knew Cecile had the hundred grand with her. The other two didn't know, at least they said they didn't. Penny the Psychic admitted to having suggested Cecile order the clams, but since she said she loved her like a sister, there didn't seem to be any obvious motivation.

Jack listened intently.

I wrapped it up and shrugged. "I don't know what to do next."

"Money seems to loom pretty large in everyone's mind here," he said. "Don't you think?"

"Yes."

"And speaking of money, they found ten grand cash in Fabrizio's room at Harry's place. Where the heck is the rest of it?"

"You're right. We kind of got derailed from that tactic, didn't we? Maybe it's time to get back to it."

We stared at each other. I didn't know about Jack, but there were at least a million things running loose in my mind all at once. Who took the money? Did the same person who took the money poison the clams? How was I ever going to become a gumshoe and do tattoos at the same time? Would I ever see the inside of my apartment again? And if not, should I keep paying my half of the rent to Cat? But most and foremost in my mind were two things: get Fabrizio out of jail and back to *la petite maison* where he belonged with Harry, and find some private time with Jack Stockton where there were no interruptions or preoccupations to distract us while we explored each other.

"Jack, I hope that once this is over, maybe we can—"

I started as something flashed just out of my line of sight, followed by a din of noise and clatter as a painting fell— no, it didn't just fall, more liked jumped—off the wall and crashed onto the hardwood floor, the frame splitting apart.

"Holy crap," Jack said, jumping up. "What caused—"

My heart had jumped into overdrive and was kicking like engine pistons. "It's Alphonse." I didn't want to admit it, but the time had come.

"It's who?" Jack picked up the impressionist watercolor of a rainy day on Bourbon Street and leaned it up against the wall. He stood, his back to me, squinting at the picture hanger, which I could see from where I sat looked perfectly fine.

"Alphonse Villars," I said. "He keeps knocking paintings off the wall."

"But there's no one here but us." He looked at me like a few of my cookies might have crumbled. "And who's Alphonse Villars?"

I went to the closet and pulled the painting of the old boy out, standing it in front of me. "This is Alphonse."

"But he's…"

"Dead. I know. About a hundred seventy-five years or so. But it's him knocking down that painting. It just makes sense that Alphonse is unhappy about something."

Jack looked at me. It seemed pretty obvious he thought the concept of a man deceased over a hundred and fifty years being unhappy didn't make any sense at all. "It isn't the first time, is it?"

I shook my head. "I don't think Alphonse likes being in the closet." Hmm, in the closet. Maybe it was a metaphor. He was related to Harry, after all. "Maintenance hung that watercolor over the empty spot on the wall. This is the fourth time it's fallen down in the six nights I've stayed here. I truly think it's Alphonse."

Jack stared at the bewhiskered old geezer in the oil. "Mel, come on. You don't really think—"

"I don't know what to think," I said. "There are a lot of stories about Mystic Isle, stories from as far back as the eighteenth century—about haints and voodoo conjurings, and witchcraft and goblins, and such. I never put much store in them, but when I was growing up, I hardly heard about anything else. My grandmama is a true believer, and she'll tell you straight out."

"Why is Alphonse in the closet in the first place?"

I ducked my head as I scooted the painting of Alphonse Villars across the floor and turned it to the wall. Maybe he'd like it better out here, even if he wasn't still hanging on the wall.

"Mel?" Jack prompted. "Did you take it down?"

I turned to him and nodded sheepishly. "I did."

"But why?"

I pulled my lips into a hard line and propped my hands on my hips. "What else was I supposed to do? The old lecher kept staring at me."

CHAPTER FOURTEEN

——————

It was Saturday morning. I'd worked seven days without a break and needed one pretty bad. I woke up early. Fabrizio on my mind.

Cap'n Jack, my hero, intended to spend part of his day looking into the background of Cecile's family and friends. Since I didn't really have a game plan outlined, I decided to spend the day somewhere I could do some good, namely at St. Antoine's, where a work crew planned to assemble later that morning to spiff up thirty old pews donated by a group over in Baton Rouge. A truck was bringing them to St. Antoine's about eleven. The plan was to nail and glue the pews all nice and tight then sand and refinish them. We probably wouldn't get it all done in just one day, maybe not even in two. That would depend on how many people showed up to do the work.

I didn't have my work clothes with me, so my itinerary included a stop at my apartment to change. I'd see Cat and Satchmo and catch up on all the latest happenings in the Crescent City.

But first I had the shuttle bus driver drop me off in Gretna at the jail and went in to visit with Fabrizio. Quincy was there working on his damn report. I could barely stand to look at him, but he took pity on me and let me sit down with Fabrizio, while the guard from the other night had only allowed the video visitation.

The Great Fabrizio looked bad. His eyes were dull, with dark half-moons beneath them. His silvery hair, normally combed back to show off his widow's peak, lay flat and lifeless against his head. I knew he was in trouble when tears sprang up in his eyes, and he said, "Oh, my dear, don't even look at me. You know I don't wear orange well."

I hugged him, and he clung to me like a baby monkey. The guard cleared his throat, and I gently disengaged.

"An indictment appearance has been scheduled for Monday. Harry's barrister will be attempting to have me released on bail." He shook his head. "Harry has no money lying around for this expense. He doesn't even have the money to meet the balloon payment coming due on the remodel at The Mansion. I was working on gathering money to help him with that. And now the poor man is struggling to come up with extra money for the bond? Whatever will we do?"

"Of course, you were trying to help him with the balloon payment."

He didn't hesitate. "Yes."

"Fabrizio," I began slowly, not wanting to get to the end of my question and hear the answer. "The ten thousand they found in your room? That wouldn't happen to be how you were planning to help Harry Villars, would it?"

He looked at me in horror. "Oh, no, my dear, please tell me you don't actually believe I would steal money from that poor woman, no matter how desperate I was."

I felt terrible, like the world's worst friend. I couldn't believe I'd even asked him that. "I'm sorry." My voice sounded small and high pitched, like a child's.

He swallowed hard. "That was indeed the money I planned to get for Harry, but I planned to get it by giving that woman the best bloody séance ever held anytime, anywhere." He twisted his mouth as if the even the words were bitter." Not by stealing it."

Of course he didn't steal it. He no more stole the ten thousand than he had killed her. How could I even think such a thing? That was when it struck me. "Fabrizio, did either you or Harry happen to mention this looming balloon payment when you were interviewed by Deputy Boudreaux?" I held my breath.

He didn't answer right away, but I could see the wheels turning in his brain as he thought back. Slowly, he nodded. "Yes. I did mention it to the deputy."

Damnation. No wonder Quincy was all hot to trot to pin this deal on Fabrizio. That dear, sweet, clueless man had provided his own outstanding motive.

Well, Mel, might as well get it over with. "Fabrizio, when was the last time you happened to be out in the old boathouse?"

"Boathouse? Why, never that I can think of. I can't swim, Melanie, my dear. Why would I ever want to go out in a boat?"

* * *

I caught a taxi down to the ferry dock, and George ferried me across the Big Muddy with four holdovers from the Dead-and-Loving-It Zombie Fan Club. It seemed like all the three guys and one girl could talk about was how awesome their annual banquet had turned out to be at The Mansion, and how they wouldn't have asked for a better theme than a murder, and better yet, the victim was possibly done in by a ghost, no less.

I kept my mouth shut and tried to ignore them. But if I was honest, I was beginning to wonder if Terrence didn't kill her—he needed her…and if Billy didn't kill her—she gave him whatever he wanted…and if Rosalyn didn't kill her—while there was no love lost between the two women, I just didn't believe Rosalyn had it in her. Then who did it? That left us with two suspects: Penny the Psychic and Theodore the Disembodied. And as far as I could tell, Penny didn't have a motive. Maybe the zombie lovers were onto something after all.

A Saturday morning in mid-July and the French Quarter was buzzing like a swarm of African bees on crack. I made my way through dense crowds of sunburned tourists, my hands both firmly gripping my LeSportsac against the light-fingered locals sure to be out and about on a day with as many possible marks as this one. Two blocks northeast along Decatur past the French Market on one side and the scads of po'boy shops, restaurants, T-shirt shops, and other tourist haunts on the other—over to Dumaine Street—three blocks up to mine and Cat's place.

I walked out of the direct sunlight through the wrought iron gate and into the shady retreat and restfulness of our courtyard. The four downstairs units in our building all opened out onto it. Our landlord, Mrs. Peabody, who lived in the four-bedroom unit next to ours, was perched on the built-up brick flowerbed, pruning her geraniums, a midsummer explosion of bright red among the faded brick, dark-green shutters, and white-trimmed French doors. A magnolia tree alive with blossoms hung over two French-style wrought iron benches.

The mix of aromas was heady. It smelled like home, my home—magnolias, baking bread, garlic, and that musty, old-world sort of scent unique to *le Vieux Carré*.

I walked through the double doors of our apartment into the main room. Cat's and my place was awesome, the essence of luxury, in my book anyway, especially compared with Grandmama Ida's double-shotgun house, where Mama and me lived while I was growing up. Grandmama Ida and Granddaddy Joe lived in one side. After my daddy left for greener pastures when I was five, Granddaddy Joe eighty-sixed the tenants and moved me and Mama into the other side. Granddaddy Joe built a divider in Mama's bedroom. They put my cot, an old chest of drawers Grandmama took in trade for a perm and a cut, my box of toys, a few pegs on the wall to hang my clothes, a Princess Jasmine rug, and my small wooden easel behind the divider. It became my room.

Cat and I combined our incomes, and she chipped in part of the healthy allowance she received from her Romanian parents in Atlanta. They'd joined the ranks of the nouveau riche when they sold their European textile import business to Williams-Sonoma. As part of their sales agreement, they received a sweet discount on household furniture and design items, and our entire apartment was decked out in an upscale arts and crafts style. Without the allowance and discount contingencies, we never would have been able to afford to live in a place like that.

Cat and Satchmo were curled up on the sofa, watching Emeril Lagasse make Peach Melba.

Satchmo jumped off the sofa and came to rub up against my leg when he saw me, and Cat paused the video.

"You talk to your traitor boyfriend this morning?" I wasn't playing fair, but then again, I wasn't in a mood to play fair.

"Oh," she said, sighing. "This is all my fault now, is it?"

That was one thing about Catalina Gabor. She was not only beautiful, loyal, and intelligent, she was also in possession of more common sense than everyone else I knew put together. "Point made," I said. "Sorry. You can't help it if your boyfriend's Benedict Arnold."

"Mel, he feels real bad about having to charge Fabrizio. He told me."

"Speaking of the devil, I'm surprised he's not all snuggled up next to you since I'm not here to inhibit him."

"Funny you should say that. He's coming over later, sez he wants to hang out in his underwear and make love all over since we have the place to ourselves."

I gave her a look, and she added, "Don't worry. I'm locking your bedroom door."

She got up from the sofa, padded through the archway into the kitchen, and set her coffee cup in the sink. I followed her in. She turned and started back but stopped and stood framed in one of the two archways that led from the parlor to our gorgeous eat-in kitchen with the granite countertops. It was really annoying how stunning she looked in her pj boy-shorts and cami top with no makeup and her hair all wild around her face. On my days off under the same circumstances, if you opened the dictionary to "frumpy," a picture of me with my hair in a ponytail, in my oversized sleep shirt and socks, is probably what you'd see there. Cat always told me that was when I was my most adorable, but she was my best friend and obligated to say that.

I slipped a pod into the coffeemaker, hit the brew button, and told her about my visit with Fabrizio and how worried I was.

"If he's actually indicted on Monday, that will free up the Elway party to leave and fly back to Philadelphia. They'll be out of reach, and Fabrizio will be screwed f'true."

She agreed things were getting scary.

"I'm gonna shower then catch a bus over to Holy Cross."

"I'm heading on over to Rouses on Royal to get groceries—Quincy's beer and a couple of muffulettas for later. You need anything?"

"No, *chère*," I said. "Both Harry and Jack seem all right with me staying at The Mansion for a while, at least until this big old mess gets cleaned up. So it looks like Valentine will be feeding me for a couple of days." I grinned at her.

"Oh, my word," she said, heavy on the drama, "what a terrible inconvenience. Eating that gourmet cooking. Staying where you're with that handsome Cap'n Jack all the time. Having housekeeping come and take care of every little ol' thing you need."

She stopped abruptly, seeming to think about what she'd said. "Don't mind me, girl. I always open my mouth and put my whole foot in it. You go. You do what you have to do. Whatever it takes to get Fabrizio out of that terrible place and back where he belongs with Mr. Villars and the rest of us." She headed for her bedroom on the far side of the apartment, tossing back over her shoulder, "And when you see your mama and grandmama today at St. Antoine's, you give 'em both a big old kiss for me."

* * *

Wearing my grungiest work clothes, I caught a bus east to the Holy Cross neighborhood, where a work crew had already gathered hours earlier to work on St. Antoine's. Because I'd come all the way from the west bank, I was the last to arrive, just in time to help Mama and Grandmama Ida lay out the lunch spread they'd brought. Fried chicken, potato salad, hush puppies, and lemonade. You think that "Colonel" from Kentucky had an awesome secret recipe? Let me just say his chicken is a distant runner-up to Grandmama Ida's.

Desi Lopez walked up to me and slung one arm across my shoulders. "Hey, bella, what's shakin'?"

"Oh, you know, Desi, another day, another fifty cents."

Desi Lopez de Monterra was a local piano player. He worked the Bourbon Street bars and hotel lounges in the Quarter, everything from Scott Joplin to Ludwig Van Beethoven. Desi was half-Cuban, half-Creole. He was smallish, on the skinny side, but every inch a ladies' man. His mocha-latte skin was the envy of every woman who knew him.

Desi was good people. I'd known him to be out on a gig until the wee hours of the morning then turn right around and head to St. Antoine's to paint, or dig, or whatever work was planned for the day.

In his free hand he held a paper plate piled high with my grandmama's chicken. He leaned over the table and pinched her papery cheek. "Sweet Ida, mamacita, maybe you can see 'bout finding a man another glass of that nice cold lemonade?"

Grandmama giggled. A rare occurrence. She was known to snicker, harrumph, or laugh out loud. But only Desi ever made her giggle.

Father Brian came up behind me, his blue eyes full of humor, and handed me a bottle of stain, a bucket of shellac, a paintbrush, a tack cloth, and several sheets of sandpaper. I took them one by one until my arms overflowed with stuff.

"Just in time, girl." He smiled his wide smile and cocked his grey shaggy head to one side. "I knew you'd show up here sooner or later. I can always count on you, Melanie, and you know every time you show up here you're piling up frequent flyer miles in Heaven."

I laughed. Father Brian was good at making people laugh. When Katrina washed out our beautiful church, I had just graduated from high school and was looking for a high-dollar fine arts and graphic arts program on a nearly nonexistent budget.

Father Brian had only been at St. Antoine's a few months and had more trouble than he could shake a stick at, what with half his church floating down river. Yet he somehow managed to find the time, energy, and patience to help me send a résumé and letter to Loyola University in my own sweet hometown and to help me navigate my way through the myriad of grants and scholarships once I was accepted there. His generous, loving nature was a good part of the reason I showed up at St. Antoine's to help whenever I possibly could and why I gave as much extra pocket money as I could come up with to help the members buy building materials to restore the church. The other part was how much St. Antoine's Parish contributed to the community and its great need.

Because I had no hands left, he reached around me and fastened a paper mask over my nose and mouth, turned me around, and sort of shoved me in the general direction of where all the work was being done on the new pews.

Within a half hour my hair, face, and clothes were covered in sanding dust. I was sweaty, and all that grit was turning into paste on my face and arms. The wax-on, wax-off motion I'd been doing on my hands and knees would have me moving funny tomorrow.

It was hard work, but Grandmama and some of the other older ladies kept coming around with pitchers of lemonade, and Desi's boom box blasted out upbeat Harry Connick Jr. tunes to keep us moving along.

I was tired and couldn't wait to go home and have a shower. I figured I must have looked like hell, but who cared—nobody was going to see me looking like this. It wasn't like any prospective boyfriends were going to show up or—

"Melanie?"

I knew that voice.

"There you are."

Really? Just shoot me now.

I looked up and—yessiree—there stood Cap'n Jack looking spectacular in a pair of black jeans, black suede chukka boots, and a grey tie-dyed Henley that fit him like he was born in it, with the sleeves pushed up on his forearms. I, on the other hand, looked like a really dusty bag lady.

Just perfect.

"Hi," I said, sitting back on my heels.

He smiled and reached down for my hand, helping me to my feet. I couldn't meet his eyes. I probably looked like the sole survivor of some freakish wall of dust in the middle of the Sahara Desert.

"Jack," I mumbled. "I'm...surprised to see you here."

He grinned, that lopsided grin that always went straight to my heart. A light came into his eyes, and it occurred to me maybe I wasn't as horrific a sight as I originally thought.

He lifted his hands and gently pulled down the disposable paper mask that covered my face from the bridge of my nose to my chin. His grin broadened. "I knew you were under there somewhere."

Self-conscious, I pulled the bandana off my head and ran my fingers through my hair, promptly depositing all the grit from hands to my scalp. Forget the shower—I'd have to walk through a car wash at the very least.

"It's just incredible what you do here, Mel," he said. "I'm so proud of you."

I think I stood up a little straighter and pulled back my shoulders, just out of pleasure.

"Harry Villars mentioned how you do this on your time off. I have to tell you it's one of the reasons I've sought you out. I was really intrigued by a young woman whose main interest isn't shopping or hair salons or gossip."

He caught me by surprise again. I didn't know what to say, and he seemed to sense it.

"Can you take a short break?" he asked. "I've learned some things I think you'll find interesting, to say the least."

CHAPTER FIFTEEN

———

I went to find Father Brian, who lay prone on the concrete floor, drill whirring madly as he and two others installed the pulpit sent over from a parish in Baton Rouge he'd had refinished last week, the week before all this craziness started at The Mansion.

When I introduced Jack, Father Brian turned off the drill and reached up from the floor to shake Jack's hand.

"Do you mind if I take a quick break, Father?" I asked. "There's new information on the murder." I knew someone was bound to have told him about the goings-on over at Mystic Isle.

Father Brian's eyes lit up. "Excellent. I always say nothing gets your blood up like a good homicide investigation." He seemed to realize what that sounded like, so he added, "Not that I endorse homicides, mind you..."

Jack, smooth as silk, handled it just right. "I like a good mystery myself, Father. And, like me, I'm sure you prefer yours to be fiction."

Father Brian sort of saluted, which made me wonder if I'd ever called my boss Cap'n Jack in front of him, then he turned the drill back on and went back to work on the base of the pulpit.

Jack and I walked outside and stopped under the shade of the sole surviving magnolia tree on the church property. The lush scent of magnolia blossoms hung in the air like perfume. Jack sat down on the grass and pulled me down beside him.

I went easily, even if thoughts of chiggers and mosquitos weren't far from my mind. Being with him was the important thing, and I didn't want to spoil the moment by bringing up the issue of itchy welts that would drive even a nun to cursing, not to mention West Nile virus.

"I called an old…" He paused, seeming to search for the right word. "An old friend who moved from NYC to Philadelphia a couple of years back. She used to be on the job in Manhattan and now works for Philly PD."

She? My she-bitch radar went to DEFCON 1.

"Your policeman friend is a woman?" I prayed my voice didn't reveal the jealousy brewing in my heart.

Ah-ha! Not a friend, a *girl*friend.

He didn't seem to notice I was turning green. His voice was matter of fact. "We used to date some when she lived in the City. She moved down to Philly to get married."

Hallelujah.

"I asked her to see what she could find on Theodore Elway's death."

I held my breath as he absentmindedly took hold of my hand and began to rub his thumb over it. At first I nearly pulled back, wondering how he could possibly expect me to concentrate on what he had to say while he was touching me. But the sensation was so pleasurable I forced myself to concentrate on his words.

"The official cause of Theodore Elway's death was listed as acute myocardial infarction."

"Heart attack. Right?"

He nodded. "But there were questions. He was known to carry nitro tablets at all times. The report indicated his daughter was suspicious that there were three bottles in his room and two in his car—all empty. The coroner found traces of Viagra in his system."

I stared at him. "That's why Rosalyn believed Cecile killed him. I don't believe men with bad tickers are supposed to fool with those little blue pills. Do you?"

He just looked at me then smiled. "I don't know. I haven't ever had to take one."

I looked away from the twinkle in his eyes. "Did your…friend…say whether or not it ever went any further than just the suspicion Cecile might have had something to do with her husband's death?"

He shook his head. "They didn't have anything substantial, just the usual variety of police suspicion and the rantings of his daughter."

"So, if Rosalyn truly believed her father died from some crazy plan Cecile put into motion, she's the person with the most motivation."

He nodded then said, "There's more. Harry Villars stopped in my office this morning. He hired a private investigator a few days ago to check into Theodore Elway's finances."

The dampness from the grass was soaking into my jeans, and my butt was getting cold, but I didn't want to get up. It was so nice sitting there with him.

"This detective is checking into the trust Elway set up for his family. It seems the old man was a miser who hung on to every penny until Lincoln started reciting his Gettysburg Address. Elway wasn't just rich—he was megarich. The estate's holdings are valued at over half a billion dollars. Once he remarried, he named Cecile Elway as administrator of the family trust, which evidently pissed off the rest of the family and was part of the reason Rosalyn was so sure Cecile had something to do with the old boy's demise."

I mulled it over. This was getting complicated. So Rosalyn had good reason to get rid of her stepmother, namely, more than 500 million reasons.

"Wow, Jack, you're good at this," I said.

He smiled and lifted his free hand. "You've just got a little something..." He lightly brushed at my cheek, his touch so feather soft I shivered.

He stood, and still holding my hand, pulled me to my feet.

It was one of those moments. He looked down at me. I looked up at him. It could have gone further—it could have been divine.

But we were standing in front of St. Antoine's and had an audience of about twenty or twenty-five others who for some reason chose that exact time to take their own break, hang around out front, and watch us.

It was easy to tell who the ringleaders were. Grandmama Ida and Mama were coming straight at us, each holding a glass of lemonade.

No necking, at least not now.

"Mama," I said. "Grandmama Ida."

It was kind of embarrassing the way those two gushed and simpered over Jack, like they were fourteen or fifteen years old and still pimply-faced and hormonal.

When Jack and Mama shook hands, she didn't let go.

"All right, Mama. All right. That's enough. He can tell you like him." I tugged their hands apart.

While she watched him down the lemonade that was so cold the glass was sweating, Mama leaned in close and whispered, "Oh, my, Melanie, this one's a keeper—don't run this one off."

"Mama!"

Oh, swell. From the expression on Jack's face, it was obvious he'd heard her, but what happened next was unbelievable. He tucked my hand in the crook of his arm, handed Mama back the empty glass, and gave her one of those swashbuckler smiles. "I'm not going anywhere, Mrs. Hamilton." He turned to me. "Let's go back inside and see if they need any help."

As we walked away, I looked back to see Mama and Grandmama holding hands and dancing in a circle.

Jack never looked at me, but he patted my hand and kept walking.

Mama was right. He was a keeper.

* * *

Once we were back inside, Jack gallantly went to Father Brian and asked if there was anything he could to do to help since he was there.

A squeegee and bucket of soapy water were handed over, and Jack was offered the title of Sparkle and Shine Specialist.

Even though he was ever so gracious about it, I figured it was more work than he had in mind. I could also tell by the dubious way he looked at the squeegee it might have been the first time he'd ever used one.

Father Brian brought around a ladder and leaned it up against the wall. He shook Jack's hand and walked away.

Jack stood there for a minute looking up before he hooked the bucket over one arm and began to climb. I forced myself to return to my own work, even though I was a little nervous about leaving Jack unsupervised with a ladder and a bucket of water. He was a grown man—how much trouble could he get into? Sure, New York City had those crazy guys who hung off the tops of tall buildings, washing windows like Spider-Man, but even a white-collar guy like Jack had to have washed a few windows in his day.

I might have been wrong about that. It wasn't more than fifteen minutes before a crash and clatter outside brought a lot of us running to see my beautiful boss sitting in a muddy puddle on the ground, soaking wet, clutching the handle of the empty bucket in one hand.

I tried to be serious as I rushed over, but, aw, he was so cute, I don't think I managed to keep from smiling.

"You hurt?" I relieved him of the bucket.

He shrugged and looked up at me sheepishly. "Just my pride."

The storm front that had been forecasted all week finally hit, and the heavens opened up. We all ran inside the church, and Father Brian called an end to our workday a little before three o'clock.

Jack called for a taxi, and I hitched a ride with him to my and Cat's place.

"Wanna come in?" I was shy about asking.

He peeled off a few bills from his money clip and jumped out of the car. "Yes." He wasn't shy about answering.

Jack had never really dried off from dumping the bucket over onto himself—plus we were both freshly soaked from the downpour by the time we made it through the courtyard to the front door. The wind was coming up some, too, by then.

Cat and Quincy were curled up on the sofa eating popcorn and watching one of the *Fast and Furious* movies on

TV. Their bare legs were entwined, and they didn't even look up when we came in until I called, "Jack's here."

Then Cat jumped up, giving me one of those *attagirl* looks as she hurried into the bathroom, coming back with two big fluffy towels.

While we dried off, she went to the fridge and came back with a bottle of Heineken that was already sweating in the humid air.

He took it and thanked her.

"Make yourself comfortable," I said to him. "I've got to get this tacky sawdust off me. Going to take a shower."

I could have strangled Cat as she called after me, "Alone?"

*   *   *

Jack and I didn't hang around long. It was awkward with Quincy there, and I could tell he and Cat were hungry for some alone time.

The storm revved and decelerated, and the rain had gone back to a soft drizzle, and it was romantic walking along Decatur Street sharing an umbrella with Jack. He didn't seem as affected by my close presence as I was by his, but he was a cool city boy, and who knew what got him stirred up? But me, I was so distracted by him I could hardly walk, much less carry on a conversation.

In the once-again rising wind, the river was choppy, and—oh, what a shame—I had to hang on to Jack to stay upright on the lurching flat-bottom boat.

Jack had phoned ahead, so the resort bus was waiting when we docked—part of the perks of traveling with the general manager, I guess. Even so, I looked like a drowned rat when I climbed aboard and sat shivering as the bus rocked and rolled to avoid major potholes and mud puddles. We had to stop once for a family of raccoons crossing the road and three times for gators. The driver even had to get out once and drag one small gator, which had stopped for a snooze, off the road by the tail. So by the time the bus pulled up under the portico, it was almost seven o'clock. Even under the protection of the overhang, the wind howled and pushed at us like the hand of some vengeful spirit. I couldn't help but think of Theodore Elway.

Bolts of lightning filled the darkened sky with fingers of electricity, and the accompanying thunder shook the very ground. Jack and I looked at each other. His eyes were wide.

"Your first summer storm here?" I asked.

His mouth was open. His eyes were wide. He nodded.

I reached up and put my hand on his shoulder. "Don't worry, Jack. This is nothing, not even a real storm."

"This isn't what you call a 'real storm?'"

My turn to be cool. "This isn't much more than a spring shower. Wait'll we get hit with a cat five hurricane."

He gulped and just looked at me. "Let's go inside."

All the guests were hanging out in the public rooms of the hotel since they couldn't go outside. It was crowded.

Based on what Jack had learned about the Elway family trust and administrative line of succession, we had decided talking to Rosalyn was a good idea since she'd moved up on our list in Cecile's murder, due not only to her suspicions her stepmother did away with her father but also because she likely resented Cecile being named executor of the trust funds.

But first, I had to get out of my soggy clothes, comb my hair, and put on some makeup—Jack, too. Well, maybe not the hair or makeup part.

We agreed to meet back at the reception desk at eight o'clock to look for Rosalyn.

Back in my room I texted Cat and told her when she came to work tomorrow to leave early since the road was such a mess, and then I raided the minibar for a bit of warmth and fortification from a teeny-tiny bottle of Amaretto. It hit bottom then radiated out, warming me from the inside out. The only clothes I'd brought besides the sundress for the party were a pair of cutoffs, which I threw on with flip-flops and a T-shirt. I hadn't expected the clean clothes I wore from home to get such a drenching.

At a few minutes to eight, I headed out to the reception desk to wait for Jack. The lights flickered, and everything went black. I'm not kidding. For at least a minute, I couldn't even see my hand in front of my face. I moved closer to the wall and began to crab-step down the hall, one hand against the wall just in case.

My hand found something soft and warm and fuzzy with a bare spot on one side—a bare spot I recognized because I was the one who shaved all the hair off to ink a happy little gargoyle with big ears and bat wings. "Oh, hello, Mr. Kendrick."

"Is that you, Melanie? What's…?"

"Don't worry. The security lights will come on in a minute, and we'll have full power from the generator in ten or twenty minutes. Best if you just stay in your room unless you hear from management."

He shut the door, and I moved on, finally coming to a stop at the reception desk as the lights came back on, just in time to see Lurch taking a selfie of his grim self with a lit flashlight under his chin.

For the next ten minutes or so, the generator struggled, thrusting the resort into blackness every minute or so. It was unsettling. Creepy. I didn't like it much. The cry of the wind brought banshees and wolves to mind. The enormous crystal chandelier in the center of the twenty-foot ceiling swayed as gusts seeped in through the ancient joints. The tinkling glass sounded like icicles shattering. Sheets of lightning spread over the sky, illuminating the main lobby. I looked up as a horrible shape loomed above me.

My heart jumped into my throat. I threw my hands up in front of my face and shrieked.

The lights came back on, and the carved gargoyle clinging to the central pillar laughed down at me, his big ears and freaky little face ridiculing me. I caught my breath and flipped him off as a firm hand landed on my shoulder, giving me yet another start.

"Ha! Gotcha!"

I turned around to see Penny Devere, hair plastered against her head, water beading up on her shiny face. Her clothes were spotty wet, not soaked through like she'd been outside, but more like someone had thrown a bucket of water on her.

"Miss Devere," I said. "Were you outside?"

She didn't answer right away. "Uh, sure."

But she didn't seem sure.

"It's raining," she said.

Duh.

"Something I can do for you, Miss Devere?"

"For starters, you can call me Penny, and then you can spend a few minutes with me. I'm worried about Rosalyn, and I know you've spent a bit more time with her than the others here."

"Oh." I looked around. The generator seemed to have settled down. The lights had quit flickering and were steady, and there was still no sign of Jack. "Let's go into the salon."

I led her through the lobby to the big room, which was nearly empty except for a couple of women lighting candles around the room. Better safe than sorry, and the warm flickering ambiance gave the big room a cozy feeling.

"Wine?" I asked.

She nodded, and I brought two glasses. One for her, one for me. "So tell me, Penny. What is it you wanted to tell me?"

She looked so serious. "Theodore, Mr. Elway, has been gone almost two years now. Back when he passed, Rosalyn went completely to pieces. She quit eating, bathing, even began to wander the house at night. She swore her father came to her from beyond the veil and told her poor Cecile had conspired to kill him."

According to what Jack told me he learned, Rosalyn wasn't the only one who had her suspicions about the way Theodore Elway died. Even the police had questions about where his heart pills were and why a man in his alleged condition would take Viagra.

"I've talked to Rosalyn," I said. "And I didn't see any signs of lunacy." Unless you counted the fact she believed the ghost of her father murdered her stepmother and that now she was being haunted by the ghost of her stepmother. But I didn't mention that to Penny because I wanted to hear everything she had to say without being prompted.

"It was so bad Cecile, God rest her soul, wanted to have her sent away to a sanitarium for a while—just until she was better, of course."

"Oh, of course."

Jack and Odeo walked in from outside, both carrying flashlights and wearing dripping rain gear. They'd probably been out to check on the generator.

Our eyes met across the room with one of those *later, baby* looks, and I caught my breath as Penny went on. "Of course, Rosalyn is much better now."

That was when a horrific shriek filled the lobby, drowning out the sound of the wind and the rain and the many voices of the folks gathered in the main lobby.

"Save me! Save me! Don't let her get me. Oh. My God!"

I turned, and the sight that met my eyes was like something out of a Scooby-Doo cartoon. Rosalyn Elway Whitlock, dressed in what I could only call a granny gown, feet bare, hairs in curlers, came racing down the grand stairway, arms flying above her head, screaming her head off.

"She's after me! Cecile's after me."

Yeah. Right. She was much better.

I heard Lurch's long, miserable groan and Jack's sudden intake of breath from behind me.

Before anyone could stop her, Rosalyn blasted across the lobby and out the open front door.

CHAPTER SIXTEEN

Jack yelled, "What the—" and he and Odeo turned and sprinted out after Rosalyn.

I turned and ran after them, out the front door into the storm. The wind drove the stinging rain into my face as I crossed the driveway onto the muddy lawn, slipping in the mushy soil. The area was well lit, but the wind-driven rain distorted my field of vision until all I could see were blurry apparitions running away from the building toward the pond.

Jack drew even with Rosalyn and caught her by the arm, turning her toward him. She threw back her head and yelled into the night, her voice rising above the sounds of the storm. Then she drew back her free arm and swung. Jack stumbled away, and Rosalyn ran on.

I ran up as Odeo helped Jack to his feet. The three of us took off after her again and, from the lights positioned on the dock pilings, could see her run out midway to where several small boats were tethered.

"Mrs. Whitlock!" Jack's call was swallowed up by the wind. He didn't stop.

Just as the three of us hit the dock, the small boat Rosalyn had commandeered drifted away in the turbulent water and was carried out toward the middle of the pond by the choppy waves.

Jack, Odeo, and I stopped at the end of the dock. Jack and I both cupped our hands around our mouths and yelled for her to come back. "It's too dangerous!"

"Well, hell," Penny's voice was beside my ear. I turned to see her standing behind me under an umbrella held by Lurch, who looked like the ferryman Charon after a dip in the River

Styx. Penny was high and dry while the rest of us were beginning to prune. "If I have my guess, I'd say she's losing it again."

Ya think? I wiped the rain out of my eyes.

"What's wrong with her?" Jack shouted.

Penny took hold of Lurch's wrist and moved the umbrella closer. "I can't imagine why she'd get in a boat like that," she hollered above the wind. "She can't swim a lick."

"She what?" Jack leaned closer to her.

"She. Can't. Swim."

Jack and I looked at each other in horror, rain running down our faces. We turned and looked out to where Rosalyn's small boat was being tossed around as she struggled to start the motor.

Jack didn't hesitate but went straight to a second small boat and jumped in. When he turned and saw I was right behind him, he reached for the piling where the boat was moored. He held it steady while I climbed aboard, and he then pulled the rope from the piling and bent to the motor.

It wouldn't start either, and while I stood there trying to figure out what to do, he picked up the oars and put his back into taking the boat out into the middle of the pond.

Hmm. "Not bad for a city boy," I said, loud enough for him to hear.

He shouted above the wind. "I have a friend who lives in the Hamptons. Used to take her boat out on her family's private lake all the time."

Her? Dammit! How many exes did he have anyway?

We made a wide turn then headed straight to the middle of the pond. Out in the open, the wind was stronger and blew the rain sideways. It stung my eyes as I peered into the darkness where Rosalyn's blurry figure still crouched in the pitching boat, waving frantically.

Jack and I didn't speak, both of us obviously concentrating on reaching Rosalyn before anything terrible happened.

And we almost did.

We were only about fifteen or so feet away when Rosalyn stood suddenly. The boat, went over, sending Rosalyn into the water head first, arms and legs in the air, her voice rising above the whistling wind.

Before I could think or even react, Jack yanked off first one shoe then the other and dove in. My heart swelled with a sense of admiration, even though it was pounding like a bass drum.

"Jack," I shouted, "be careful!"

He didn't look back, his strong arms slicing through the inky water. I looked around—did gators go to ground during storms, or did they slink around in the water looking for post-dinner snacks? Jack and Rosalyn were stirring things up, and if there was a gator out and about, he'd surely notice the ruckus they were making.

Her head went under. *Oh, Jack. Hurry.*

And as if he heard my thoughts, he seemed to swim faster, and as her head ducked a second time, he reached out midstroke, grabbed her by the hair, and pulled, yanking out some of her curlers, until he could take hold of the granny gown, which had probably wrapped itself around her legs and conspired to help drown her.

Now it became an instrument of her salvation as Jack twisted it around one arm while wrapping the other around her shoulders under her chin. He seemed to be an extremely strong swimmer, and in only a couple of minutes, they were within reach of my little boat, which rocked wildly. I spread my weight as evenly in the middle as possible, arms stretched side to side, but the rocking just got worse.

Jack and Rosalyn were within a few feet. Even in the darkness of the rainy night, I could see he was having trouble with her. She was obviously in full panic mode, her arms flailing as she tried to grab Jack around the neck. Her kicking feet kept coming to the surface.

Jack was having trouble keeping his own head above water. He brought her up beside the boat. "Knock it off," he yelled at her. "You're going to drown us both."

And he was right. His head went under as she tried to lift herself over him onto the boat. I moved to one side and leaned over, reaching out with both arms. And wouldn't you know it, that nut job grabbed me with one hand, the side of the boat with the other, and yanked.

And me? I went headfirst into the cold, smelly pond water, splashing through the thick duckweed, my shoes and clothing pulling me straight down.

Above me, Jack's legs stilled as if he were aware I was directly beneath them. He reached one arm down, but just as our hands nearly met, one of Rosalyn's feet connected with my head. Hard, but I didn't black out and still had enough of my wits about me to keep my mouth shut.

I was aware of a frantic struggle going on above me. Rosalyn was kicking like a mule and pushing on Jack to try and lift herself into the boat. They were churning up the water like two gators fighting over a fat little muskrat while I sank deeper into the murky pond. It grew darker, and quieter, and even though I realized what was happening wasn't good, not only did I not do anything about it, I didn't care. It was calm down there. Peaceful even. I could just relax and float and...

A hand—at least it seemed like a hand reached for me. The voice, present and clear, said, "Kick, Mellie gal, kick hard."

Oh. Of course. I reached up, just missing the lowered hand and put my feet in motion in one hard thrust after the next.

My hands found the edge of the boat. My head broke water, and suddenly Jack was beside me, lifting me up. "Pull, Mel," he said, his voice strong and authoritative but somehow different than the voice in the water.

It only took a couple of minutes, or at least that was what it seemed like, for him to get Rosalyn, me, and himself situated in the boat. He put his back into the oars again, and our small craft headed toward the dock.

CHAPTER SEVENTEEN

Odeo and two other workers ran up. Jack threw them the rope, and they looped it over the piling and then helped the three of us out of the boat.

Penny and Lurch were nowhere in sight. Rosalyn seemed awfully shaky, so Odeo picked her up as easily as if she were a three-year-old and carried her back toward the main building.

I stood shivering on the dock, confused, somewhat dazed, until Jack turned to me, tipped up my chin, his dark eyes gleaming in the feeble light. "Are you okay?"

My voice wasn't ready to make a debut yet, so I just nodded.

His eyes softened as he pulled duckweed from my hair and flicked it from his fingers into the water.

"I smell like a sewer," I said and started to cry.

He smiled, put an arm around me, and said, "Me, too. We should start a club. Let's get back inside and wash the *eau de bayou* down the drain."

* * *

Back in the lobby, Jack asked Lucy, the agent on desk duty, to call Billy Whitlock's room and get him downstairs to help his mother. Odeo put Rosalyn down and led her to a bench. She sat and looked up at him with grateful eyes.

Lurch stood in the open doorway, shaking himself like a big ol' wet dog and drying his cell phone with his shirttail, while Penny marched over to Rosalyn and laid into her. "Just when I was telling everyone how much better you are, you have to go and make me look like a fool. What were you thinking, screaming through the place like that? And what in the blue blazes made you think you could handle a boat?"

Rosalyn reached up and took hold of both of Penny's hands, shaking them. "Come to my room with me. Please. You don't understand. I'm telling you—she's after me. Cecile."

Penny shook her loose and stepped back, shaking her head. "Cecile's dead, Rosalyn. And I'm the psychic here. If Cecile's spirit was going to contact anyone, don't you think it would be me?"

One of the women on housekeeping night duty came with several blankets and passed them out.

"Well..." Jack turned speculative eyes in my direction. "You heading off to your room for a hot shower?"

"I..." Stuttering, swell. But the look he was giving me absolutely made me wonder if he was waiting for an invitation to join me there. That sounded good to me as well—after all, the man *had* saved my life. "Thank you for saving me, Jack."

"I just helped you into the boat. You pretty much saved yourself, Mel. And it was a good thing too. Rosalyn was so freaked out, I thought she was going to drown us both. I had my hands full just handling her."

"But you did reach down for me, when you told me to kick—and then you helped me grab onto the side of the boat?"

He frowned and laid his hand against my upper arm, curling his fingers lightly around it. "Are you sure you're okay? I mean, she kicked you, right? In the head?"

"What?" I said, suddenly uncomfortable.

"I didn't reach for you, Mel," he said kindly. "No one did. I barely got Mrs. Whitlock over the side of the boat when you burst to the surface and latched on to the side. I didn't reach down for you. You reached up."

I just stared at him. "No. You took my hand." Didn't he? If it wasn't Jack then...maybe I was more confused than I thought.

But no matter. Cap'n Jack had saved me from the murky deep, and I wanted to spend the night wrapped in his arms. "Jack, I—"

Rosalyn's shrill voice interrupted what could have been a pivotal moment in my life. "It was her! I swear it. Cecile. She thinks I killed her. She's after me, I tell you."

Billy Whitlock came stumbling down the stairs singing "All About That Bass" and began to waltz with the young woman from housekeeping. His slack mouth, lack of focus, and unsteadiness were red flags that he'd spent the night at the bar in the Presto-Change-o Room, throwing back hurricanes.

After a few minutes he noticed his weeping mother, went to sit beside her, and began to remove what few curlers were left hanging in her wet and tangled hair.

She whimpered and laid her head on his shoulder. "Billy, let me stay with you tonight. I'm afraid."

"Stay?" he mumbled. "With me? I'm planning on hooking up." He stood so abruptly Rosalyn nearly fell off the bench. She threw her arms around his waist and started to cry all over again.

"Geez, Mother." He pried her hands off him. "You're killing me here. Can't you see I'm making my moves? You need to knock it off and go do something about my bar bill. The house says they're cutting me off if I don't take care of it."

She sniffled. "Bar bill? Don't you have a credit card, sweetie?"

"Yeah, I *have* a credit card, but it's maxed out. And I drained my checking account before we came down here. Just handle it, will ya, Mother? I've got bigger fish to fry." He winked and staggered back to where the girl from housekeeping stood waiting for any further requests. He began to flirt with her— well, sort of. In reality it was more like a dog sniffing around a steak. From the look on her face, he wasn't going to get lucky, at least not with her, at least not tonight, but he didn't seem to notice.

Rosalyn turned her pleas to Penny. "Can I stay in your room tonight, Penny? Or could you stay with me?"

Penny crossed her arms, her posture and expression completely disgusted. "Don't be ridiculous. Get yourself together, and go to bed. If you're not careful, someone's going to call a sanitarium."

That sent Rosalyn into fresh waves of sobbing and shaking. "I'm frightened. So frightened. I can't be alone tonight. She'll come for me. I know she will."

I couldn't take it anymore. I sat down beside Rosalyn and put my arm around her. "I'll stay in your room with you tonight, Rosalyn." I looked up at Jack. The expression on his face was…what? Regret, maybe? But he gave me a small nod of encouragement. "I don't blame you, Rosalyn. If Cecile's ghost is wandering around The Mansion, I'm not too crazy about sleeping alone either."

But sleeping in her bed wasn't exactly what I had in mind.

* * *

Rosalyn waited in my room while I took a hot shower then threw my sleep shirt and toothbrush into a bag. We went straight up to her room, a junior suite, which made my standard room look like a broom closet.

Rosalyn left the door open while she showered, steaming up the bedroom where I stretched out in the king-size bed watching *The Tonight Show* while Jimmy Fallon and Kevin Hart smashed eggs against their heads.

A fresh flannel nightie, her hair smelling like shampoo, she crawled into bed with me after taking three extra pillows from the closet and lining them up between us.

Don't worry, sweetie. You're not my type.

The poor thing must have been as exhausted as I was, because she was already snoring softly as I drifted off to sleep. In the back of my mind were questions about why Billy was so broke he couldn't even pay his bar bill, while he'd sworn, "I had the old biddy wrapped around my pinky," and "When I needed money, she was Johnny-on-the-spot with the checkbook."

I didn't know what time it was, but something was wrong—like when you wake up in the middle of the night because there's water dripping in a sink, or the ceiling fan starts creaking, or sometimes even just a shift in the atmosphere of the room sends your Spidey-sense on full alert.

Well, that was what happened to me. And it was a darn good thing it did, too.

I opened my eyes and was suddenly aware Rosalyn was sitting up in bed with the sheet pulled over her head, whining.

Understandable.

Because floating at the foot of the bed was a ghoul—a girl ghoul, at least, I think. Its hair was long and stringy, as much spiderwebs as anything else. Its face was skeletal in appearance with hollow sockets where the eyes should have been and bared teeth in a lipless mouth. Under a gauzy robe-like gown, an unholy light shown from its chest up onto its horrible glowing face. Its cry went straight to my very core, gripping me in an icy thrall that matched the specter's long bony fingers.

"Holy shit!" I dived under the covers too. It seemed like a good idea at the time.

Close beside me but separated from me by the stupid pillow barrier, Rosalyn's breath was fast and shallow.

"Make it go away!" she whispered. "Get rid of it!"

Sure. No problem. Let me just get my handy-dandy proton gun, maybe even cross the streams.

The ghost began to wail in a guttural alto. "Rosalyn, Rosalyn, why did you kill me? I loved you as if you were my own daughter. You broke my heart." A long, earsplitting shriek that seemed to go on awhile set my teeth on edge as every spooky tale my grandmother told me through the years leapt to the frontal lobe of my brain. Haints. Specters and spirits. Ghouls and ghosties. She had a dozen names for them, but in the end it all boiled down to the same thing—namely ugly, creepy things that can make a grown man scream like a little girl. I began to shake.

Rosalyn took hold of my wrist in a vicelike grip. "I told you. I told you she was after me."

"You were right!"

I didn't know what to do, but one thing was f'sure. I couldn't just sit there with the sheet pulled over my head.

When it came to getting rid of pesky spirits, Grandmama Ida said, "First of all, they don't always know they're dead, and they may just be hanging around waiting to make a run to Popeye's Chicken or something—so you have to tell them.

Second of all, you can't just kick them out of your house—you have to host an intervention from the other side by the haint's family members. Be sure to tell the haint to go into the light so it doesn't just boogie on over to your neighbor's house. Third, burn some sage sticks and spread the smoke by walking counterclockwise around here and there. And fourth, make sure you're stone-cold sober while you're doing this, or the haint may just take the opportunity to make that chicken run in your body."

"We have to send her to the light," I whispered to Rosalyn. "You don't happen to have any sage lying around, do you?"

Even in the dim light I could see she was looking at me like all my dogs weren't barking. "Sage? What are you talking about?"

The ghost's moaning and wailing grew louder. Was it getting closer? I couldn't tell without looking, and I wasn't ready to do that just yet.

It was a shame about the sage—would really have liked to have it, but you work with what you've got.

My voice shook like a high-rise during a Richter eight earthquake. "Ghost, er, lady…we need to let you know that, well, you're dead, girl. Six feet under, kicking up daisies, bought the farm—dead. And you need to go into the light." I turned to Rosalyn. "You think there's a light? I didn't see one. You think she sees one?"

Rosalyn shrugged. A lot of help she was turning out to be.

"It is time to leave here, all is well. There is nothing here for you now. Go into the light. Gooooo. Intoooo. The. Liiiiight. Farewell."

There was a thump, followed by a soft "Oooof." Then nothing.

Oooof? Really? Did it run into the pearly gates going into the light?

Rosalyn and I looked at each other. I could barely see the shine of her eyes. "You think it's gone?"

"Only one way to tell." I took in a deep breath and held it then slowly pulled the sheet back off my head.

Rosalyn didn't move.

I looked around. All around, and slowly exhaled. The room was empty. No more ghost.

I touched Rosalyn's shoulder. "All gone."

She let the sheet slide off her head and looked around too.

I lifted my face and began to inhale. A familiar scent lingered in the room. Clean, rich, nutty. Like almond cookies. What the...? One would think ghastly ghouls from beyond the veil would reek of rotting flesh and decay, not smell like Mama's kitchen after school.

Oh, well. I had other things to think about, like Rosalyn, who had collapsed into a quivering, weeping mess. I popped a couple of Kleenex from the box on the nightstand and handed them to her.

She wiped her eyes, and then she blew her nose.

I put my arm around her. "Well, at least they won't be calling the men in white coats to come and take you away."

She turned to look at me. Her expression still frightened—the moonlight bringing out the fear in her eyes. "Men in white coats? Someone was going to call the men in white coats?"

"Don't worry about it. At least if they do, you'll have company because they'll probably take me too."

CHAPTER EIGHTEEN

———

Sunday morning I was all set to meet Cat in the main kitchen where Valentine had promised she'd fix some extra grits, Andouille sausage, and scrambled eggs with sautéed onion. I'd been thinking about breakfast all morning.

Cat and I both had full schedules at work today, but she insisted on coming in early to help me with trying to find evidence that would exonerate Fabrizio.

Valentine plated food for us then went to go over the lunch menu with the waiters and kitchen staff.

Cat and I were both in fifty shades of ecstasy with the grits and sausage and eggs.

I told her about the fun and games she'd missed the night before, and she proposed that while she was glad she was absent for the actual events, she was also glad to be there today.

"There's something really weird about neither one of those boat motors working last night," she said.

That same thought had come to me then made a quick exit when the ghost appeared last night. "Okay. It is weird. Odeo keeps those little boats in tip-top shape. It's a matter of personal pride to him."

"So, maybe someone besides Odeo has been working on the motors."

Our eyes met over our coffee cups. "What do you think about going out to the dock to have a peek at those boats?"

With a keen look in her eyes, she took one last bite of eggs, wrapped a piece of sausage in a paper towel, and stood. "Sounds reasonable to me, sugah."

"Let's get on with it. I have a customer at ten sharp. Mr. Livermore in 220. Says he wants a kitty. A kitty. I offered him a feral cat with a high back and scorching green eyes. He turned it down. Then I said, 'What about an intricate Cheshire cat with a gorgeous sweeping kaleidoscope of a tail?' Nope, didn't want that either. 'How about a panther? You know, on the prowl, high in a vine-covered tree?' I asked him. But no, this guy wants his own kitty tattooed on his chest. It's a little bit of a calico thing with big, sad eyes, and a pink nose. Honest to gosh, Cat, it'll take me all of ten minutes to ink it. I can't believe I couldn't talk him out of it."

Cat laughed. "Can you imagine getting it on with that guy and coming face-to-face with the pussy on his chest?"

My turn to laugh. "Speaking of pussy...do you honestly think a man who puts a permanent picture of his kitty on his chest is ever going to get laid?"

We agreed it wasn't likely, went out the side door, and headed around to the lake.

* * *

There wasn't a single boat lined up at the dock.

We went inside the boathouse where we found Odeo standing in the midst of a half dozen outboard motors, hands on his hips, shaking his head, his clothes covered in grease.

"Odeo," I said. "What's going on here?"

He took his handkerchief from his back pocket and wiped his face. "Oh, lordy, Miss Melanie," he lamented. "I'm afeared what happened out dere on the lake last night wasn't no accident. Nary a drop of gas in any of these here motors."

I knew it. Cat grabbed hold of my hand in excitement. Someone was still wreaking havoc at The Mansion on Mystic Isle, and I was willing to bet it was the same someone who stole Mrs. Elway's money and then killed her. Maybe there was still a chance to save Fabrizio after all.

We left Odeo to his motors, still shaking his head, at a loss as to how someone could be so cruel as to launch an attack against such fine pieces of mechanical engineering as his boat motors.

It was about nine-thirty, and the sun was higher in the sky than before. The humidity was dense and moist, sticky. If a breeze didn't come up, it would be nearly unbearable later on in the day. I was almost glad I had a full day in the air-conditioned comfort of Dragons and Deities, except it would impede any further investigation until I fulfilled my scheduled appointments.

"One thing I don't get," Cat said as we crossed the lush green lawn to the front door.

"Just one thing?"

"So someone drained all the boat motors of gasoline, thinking when Rosalyn took one she'd be adrift, which meant she might end up floating face down in the swamp."

"Mmm," I said. "I think that pretty much sums it up."

"Okay," she went on a bit hesitantly, "how did that someone know Rosalyn, who couldn't swim and would normally stay as far away from water as possible, would head straight for one of those boats?"

I stopped walking and looked at her. Well, duh. How was it I hadn't thought of that? Maybe I was just too close to it, or maybe knocking boots with Quincy was starting to rub off on her. "That's an excellent question, Cat, and the answer to it just might be the key that unlocks the door to Fabrizio's jail cell."

* * *

I still couldn't figure out why someone would come all the way out to Mystic Isle to get a tattoo of a calico kitty, a waste of my creativity if you asked me, and in the end I was able to persuade him to move the tat to his back, where it would at least swell when he flexed.

I worked through my schedule, and a few minutes after four, Cat showed up at my doorway, looking tired.

I was anxious to get back to our sleuthing, but she begged off for an hour.

"I'm scheduled for a massage," she said tiredly. "A free massage, and no way I'm going to pass it up. I really need it."

Cat never ever had to pay for one of the delicious massages at the Hidden Passage Spa. One of the masseuses there was sweet on her. But then, wasn't everyone? And since she'd probably spent most of yesterday and last night doing horizontal calisthenics with Quincy, she most likely wasn't kidding when she said she really needed it.

She stretched her arms over her head and bent at the waist, first to one side then the other. "Mmm, and afterward I'll be all slippery and loosened up and ready to help you..."

Warm and slippery, loose and ready, and slick with lotion—

"Jiminy Christmas!"

She jumped. "What? What is it?"

"Hurry," I said. "Go, go now, and get back to me as fast you can."

I took hold of her shoulders and turned her around to face down the hall toward the hidden passage that opened into Hidden Passage Spa.

Several things had occurred to me all at once. And they all had to do with Cat and her hot stone massage at the Hidden Passage Spa. One—I suddenly knew where Rosalyn's "ghost" had been hanging out and why it smelled so sweet. Two—I also knew it wasn't really otherworldly. And three—the concealed doorway to the Hidden Passage Spa wasn't the only secret corridor in the resort.

Oh, boy. "Cat, hurry," I repeated. Now that all this new information was whirling around in my brain, it seemed urgent to put it to good use.

* * *

Cat was true to her word. She found me in the Presto-Change-o Room waiting for Jack. I was anxious to tell him what I'd figured out.

She came to me exactly as she'd predicted, warm and slippery, loose and ready.

Harry Villars had the lotion they used at the Hidden Passage Spa shipped in from a hot mineral springs spa in Baden-Baden, Germany, where aristocrats had been soaking their loins for over three hundred years. The massage lotion, rich and creamy, a sesame oil base with a warm, nutty undertone of almonds was part of a basket every recipient of a spa package received to take with them. And it was exactly what lingered in the air after our ghoul's vanishing act the night before.

Rosalyn's haint and Cat smelled yummy just like that lotion, which led me to believe the visitor tormenting Rosalyn Elway Whitlock was no more from the other side than I was.

But there was yet one other piece of the puzzle involving Rosalyn we had to figure out, and Cat was quick to hone in on it.

"But what would someone—anyone—have to gain from scaring Rosalyn like that?"

"Good question." Jack had walked up behind Cat. He walked around the table, leaned down, and gave me a peck on the cheek like it was something he'd been doing for years. I nearly fell out of the chair.

Cat's eyes bugged out.

He turned a chair and straddled it, his hands folded across the back, chin resting on them. "So, what's the answer?"

Cat and I took turns explaining about the boat motors, the "haunting," the lotion. He listened without interrupting, but when we finished, he repeated the original questions. "So, what *would* someone gain from scaring Rosalyn that way, and how did the person who drained the gas from the boat motors know she'd be going out there after one?"

I thought about it and tried to remember what we knew so far about Rosalyn, about the murder and theft, about everything. "Evidently, Rosalyn has a history of mental instability, and she's in line after Cecile Elway to take over as executor of the estate and administrator of the family trust. If she were to be declared incompetent for some reason, such as seeing ghosts running around in her hotel room at night, then it stands to reason any other person named as administrator would benefit."

"Funny we should be talking about this right now," Jack said, "because I just came from speaking with Harry Villars. The private detective he hired to look into the background and finances of these people has come up with yet another interesting tidbit about the Elways."

Cat and I both leaned in to better hear over the band running their sound check.

"When Cecile first took over, she went to the family attorney and reorganized the line of succession in the trust, naming Penelope Devere to take over as administrator in the event Rosalyn was unable to perform her duties."

"Why would Cecile do that? Name her psychic?" Cat asked. "That doesn't make sense."

"Well," I said, "there obviously wasn't any love lost between Cecile and her stepdaughter, and who knows, maybe once Rosalyn started ranting and raving about her having killed Theodore, she really did think Rosalyn was nuts and wouldn't be able to serve the estate."

Cat narrowed her eyes. "It kind of scares me, but I think it's all beginning to make some sense. If Penny stands to take over the lucrative job of doling out the Elway money, it would be pretty handy to have Rosalyn institutionalized for running around screaming there are ghosts chasing her all over the place."

I reached out and touched each of them on the hand. "Holy moly, y'all. When I spoke to Penny on Thursday, she went straight from me to a massage at the spa. You guys, she would have received the lotion in the gift basket."

Jack nodded slowly. "Yes, and it even makes sense that in case you can't make someone look crazy, maybe you just drown them."

I shook my head, not wanting to disagree with Cap'n Jack and possibly hurt his feelings, but..."There's still the matter of the boat thing. I mean, come on. How could anyone possibly know someone with a deep-seated fear of water would run out and jump in a boat?"

I looked at Cat. She shrugged.

I looked at Jack. He shook his head. He didn't know either, but he pushed off the chair and stood. "I can think of the perfect person to ask about that," he said.

He grinned down at me. Ah, Jack, so cute.

"Rosalyn," he said. "We should ask Rosalyn."

CHAPTER NINETEEN

———

We came up empty-handed in our search for Rosalyn until we stopped Lurch and asked him if he'd seen her.

"I do believe I caught a glimpse of her out by the pool," he said, his voice so James Earl Jones, I expected to hear *Star Wars* dialogue.

And he was right.

Rosalyn had taken over one of the patio tables and spread her playing cards across the top. No less than four empty Collins glasses with The Mansion's signature plastic mini-buccaneer swords lying at the bottom of the glasses. She'd been drinking Captain Hooks—spiced rum, sugar, and 7UP—deceptively sweet coma-inducing libations. And from the slackness of her face and lack of focus in her eyes, she might have indulged in even more than the four empties on the table.

She looked up as we approached her table, swaying, lifting her hand to wave, as limp as a rag doll. "Excellent, Melanie, my one and only ally in this godforsaken mudhole."

Beside me, Jack sucked in his breath but didn't counter.

"Rosalyn," I said, "may we sit down?"

"Of coursh, let me just…" she slurred, sweeping the table clear with one arm. Cards flew, and plastic "pool" glasses clattered to the pool deck.

Jack flinched and motioned to one of the cabana boys, who was Johnny-on-the-spot, picking everything up off the deck. Rosalyn watched through bleary eyes, reaching out to pat the young man on the rear as he bent over picking up the mess she'd made.

Cat and I looked at each other, amused. Jack's jaw hung open.

Guess those Captain Hooks loosened her up a little.

"Rosalyn" I had to snap my fingers a couple of times to get her attention, "we have a couple of questions for you. Do you mind?"

She seemed to notice Jack for the first time and leaned over, flirting, chin on hand, until her elbow slid out from under her, that is.

We all winced as her chin hit the table, but she just smiled and propped herself back up. "Whassup, Mr. Hotel Manager?"

Jack shook his head and covered his face with his hands.

"Last night, Rosalyn," I began, noticing how her expression darkened, "there's something really important I have to tell you about last night."

She reached across the table and grabbed Jack's hand, staring desperately into his eyes. "This city is headed for a dishaster of biblical pro-por-portions. Will you save me?"

Jack looked at me and shrugged. "Sure. Why not?"

"That wasn't Cecile's ghost in your room last night."

That got her attention. She dropped Jack's hand and turned toward me.

"In fact, Rosalyn, I don't think it was anybody's ghost. Séances and haunted houses? There aren't as many of them around as you might think. They're few and far between. And I'm pretty sure the spirits hanging around don't spend their spare time in the Hidden Passage Spa getting the house lotion rubbed all over them."

Rosalyn just sat there a minute, staring at me then she blinked several times. "That's what that smell was? I never smelled it before, so I thought it was, you know, the way ghosts smell."

Cat had been hanging back, standing off to the side letting Jack and me take the lead. I motioned her over. She came and stood next to Rosalyn, whose nostrils flared. "Oh, sweet Jehoshaphat." She took hold of Cat's hand, dragged it to her nose, and took a good deep whiff. "That *is* it, isn't it?"

I nodded.

"The *house* lotion, you say?" she asked.

"It's imported special for the spa here, and as far as we know, it's not used anywhere else." I looked at Jack. "At least nowhere else around here."

Rosalyn took a minute to put it all together in her rum-soaked brain. "So whoever's been trying to drive me crazy is as mortal as I am?"

Again, I nodded.

"Well, I'll be." She looked stunned. "And who do you think it was?"

I shrugged. "We know Penny has the lotion, and Terrence."

Rosalyn frowned. "Terrence? That no-good, lying womanizer."

"You think Terrence might be up to trying to make you believe Cecile's ghost was coming after you?"

"Are you kidding?" She rang the words together, and her tongue tangled up around them. "He might even be the one who actually killed my stepmother."

I don't know about Cat and Jack, but I was afraid to speak or even move, afraid that in her state of inebriation, the poor girl might just lose her train of thought.

But she didn't. She wrapped it all up and handed it to us. "Cecile was Terrence's sugar mama. Under the guise of his Alien caterpillars, he took money from her—from us. But when she found out there was no such thing as a conservancy for the nasty little buggers, she was about to cut him off. Isn't it convenient?" It came out *covenant*. "She died before she could do it. And, isn't it just too interesting," it came out *interfering*, "I told him the night Cecile died that I'd be following her wishes and cutting him and the blasted caterpillar off at the dick."

Beside me, I thought I heard Jack gasp as he put a protective hand near his crotch.

He cleared his throat. His voice cracked at first, but he went on. "I have a question, Mrs. Whitlock."

She turned to him.

"We were told you can't swim."

"That's true," she said, batting her eyes. "I can't, which makes you my hero, Jack. If there's anything I can do to repay you for saving me…"

Well, she certainly didn't have any trouble saying that.

"We were wondering about the boat—about why a person who can't swim would get in a boat and head out to the middle of pond far too deep to stand up in."

Rosalyn blinked her red-rimmed eyes and looked up at the cabana boy arriving with a tray and yet another Captain Hook cocktail. She took a long drag through the straw. "That's easy, Mishter Stockton. There was a ghost chasing me, and everyone knows, ghosts won't go out on water. They hate the stuff."

Cat and I looked at each other and said in unison, "Who told you that?"

"Penny, of course."

Oh, of course. "She oughta know. She is psychic, after all."

* * *

We sat with Rosalyn another fifteen minutes or so while she finished off her last drink. Jack asked one of the pool girls to go walk her up to her room so she could sleep it off.

Jack had hotel business to take care of, leaving Cat and me to find Billy Whitlock even though Catalina assured me, since she'd been telling his fortune and reading his cards, she was positive he wasn't a killer. There were still a couple of things we needed to know, about Penny Devere specifically.

"Shouldn't be all that hard," Cat said, her voice drier than the Kalahari. "He's always in one of three places—the House of Cards paying for reading but the whole time just bugging me for a date, the Presto-Change-o Room soaking up hurricanes, or the Hidden Passage Spa harassing Tina while she's trying to give him a professional massage."

"Could that possibly make him our sweet-smelling haint?"

"No way," she said. "I feel it in my bones. The boy couldn't kill a fly, unless he annoyed it to death."

Sometimes I believe Cat *is* a legitimate fortune-teller.

Billy was facedown on the massage table, having a thorough going over by Tina, our gorgeous Asian masseuse with size D cups.

He rolled over at the sound of Cat's voice, and we couldn't help but notice his nether regions rise to the occasion as Tina covered him with the sheet.

Cat rolled her eyes and made it a point to stay back out of his reach.

"Billy," she said. "Mel and I need to ask you a few things."

"What's in it for me?" He was positively leering.

"If you help us out, I might not call my boyfriend and ask him to take out a restraining order against you."

"Oh," I said, nodding. "And I've heard Deputy Quincy Boudreaux has a very special way of serving those restraining orders."

"He does," Cat said. "You don't happen to have a bulletproof vest, do you, Billy?"

He smiled tightly, obviously aware we were making fun of him. "What questions?"

"What do you think of Penny Devere?"

"She's not my type."

"No, Billy. What do you know about her relationship with Cecile, and with your mother too?"

"Oh." He narrowed his eyes and wagged a finger. "What do you ladies have on your gorgeous minds?"

We waited.

He propped himself up on his elbows. "Penny was my grandfather's longtime psychic adviser. He used to call her up if the market went down or if he was in the middle of some merger or other business deal. He relied on her—a lot. There were times she was stuck to him like Velcro.

"After my grandfather died, Penny started hanging around Cecile more and more. Cecile finally started paying Penny to be *her* psychic adviser. They were both on the board of the International Paranormal Society. Cecile was the president— you know, the grand pooh-bah of the whole shebang. She got Penny nominated as vice-president and suckered her into doing all the work. I think Penny got her nose out of joint about it.

Heard them having a pretty good go-around about it one time when they didn't know I was nearby. This club thing was real important to them, to both of them, but maybe more important to Penny than to Cecile. She didn't really have anything else going for her. You know? She ain't that great to look at, and if you ask me, she's about as psychic as a boloney sandwich."

CHAPTER TWENTY

My cell phone went off, Blue Oyster Cult's "Don't Fear the Reaper." I snatched it up as the air whooshed from my lungs. It was the Jefferson Parish jail with a call from Fabrizio.

"Melanie, my dear?"

"Yes, Fabrizio, what's wrong?" I breathed.

"Nothing's wrong, my dear. Well, that isn't entirely true, is it? But on the whole, I'm in reasonably good shape. Catalina's man, Deputy Boudreaux, has been hospitable, all things considered."

"Oh." What a relief. A thousand terrible thoughts had bombarded my mind.

"I'm hoping you'll grant me a favor," he said softly.

"Oh, yes. Of course. What do you need?"

"I know it's a huge imposition, my dear, but I'm wondering if you might consider making the trip to the indictment with Harry tomorrow. He isn't in very good shape, and if things don't go as planned, I'm afraid he might need—"

I interrupted him. Since I was knee-high to a ladybug, Grandmama Ida had drilled into my head that the spoken word was a powerful weapon and that putting it out into the universe could make it manifest. I wasn't going to let Fabrizio temp fate like that.

"It's going to come good, Fabrizio," I said, my heart and soul full of hope and prayer that what I was saying was true. "The arraignment will result in them setting you free. I just know it."

He didn't speak for a moment, and when he did, his voice was flat. "Will you come with him?"

My heart broke in two. "Of course I will."

* * *

I went out to the boathouse where Odeo was working and borrowed the keys to one of the resort golf carts guests and employees used to get around the considerable acreage of the resort. I hadn't ever driven one before, but how hard could it be—especially after the crash course Odeo gave me.

Harry Villars lived on the resort grounds a ways off from the main building in what had once been the plantation office where the owner and his accountant met to review the personal, plantation, and household books.

The path to it was paved and smooth and provided no hazards unless you counted the half-dozen or so costumed women from the Covenant of Tara, a Wiccan group who gathered yearly at the resort to honor their namesake goddess, Tara, the mother goddess of unquenchable hunger that propels all life—take that, Alex Trebek. They spent their five-day retreat moseying around the grounds and sitting on the veranda eating and drinking, all day, all the time—unquenchable being the key word here. Good thing the ladies hung out in those loose, flowing robes.

They were a colorful, eclectic group, and I couldn't help but watch as they approached. I veered off to the right so they could pass, and before I knew it, the cart bumped up onto the rise of a small berm. And Jiminy Christmas! The center of gravity shifted, the right two wheels went up in the air, and I was doing a stunt worthy of a James Bond flick. I steered what little I could to keep from going completely over. The pavement was way too close to my face. The Wiccans began to gurgle and shriek, and just as I thought I was going to lose it, three of the courageous witches ran over and leveraged their weight against the cart, bringing it (and, more importantly, me!) safely down onto all four wheels. I lifted my foot off the accelerator, snapped down the brake, and jumped out to embrace them.

"Ohmigod. Thank you so much."

The women literally purred, blessed my future with "white light and smooth pavements," and went their way.

Whew. Their spell must have worked, because I made it on over to *la petite maison* without further incident.

Harry and Fabrizio's place was a smaller version of the main building, only of red brick construction instead of lumber. *La petite maison* was in the Georgian style with four Roman columns spaced across the front. A red door with white trim led the way into the one-story house.

I'd only been there once before for Harry's famous Christmas party. The medium-sized house had filled to the brim with what must have been two hundred people of all sizes, shapes, ethnicities, and economic classes. Harry was well-known as a Renaissance man with little or no prejudices unless you counted rudeness or mean-spiritedness.

His place reflected his genteel upbringing and impeccable style. Dark wood floors blanketed with Persian rugs, rich jewel tones on the walls, chandeliers from another era—a comfortable sense of home and manor.

Grandmama Ida would have drooled over the wall-to-wall antique furnishings and tchotchkes. Her traditional double-shotgun house was built in the 1920s. There was no room or money for the accumulation of things. But she did love her some of that old Southern stuff.

"My dear." Harry opened the door and stood back, obviously surprised to see me. "Won't you please come in?"

He looked bad, real bad. Unshaven, hair tousled, eyes sunken and despaired. I knew he was in big-time trouble when I noticed he was wearing, oh lord, sweatpants. But no matter how exhausted, worried, or sad he was, Harry Villars was a gracious host.

"May I get you something, Miss Hamilton? Peach-flavored iced tea? Iced latte?"

"Oh, Mr. Villars, thank you, but I'm fine. I came to ask you a favor."

"Of course, let's sit down." He led me from the lovely, light-infused foyer to a darker, but just as cozy, parlor where a lovely late nineteenth-century Haake upright piano grounded the room on one side, and a traditional marble-manteled fireplace anchored the other.

The piano top hosted dozens of photographs of Harry, Fabrizio, Harry and Fabrizio together, as well as other people I didn't recognize but who held a strong resemblance to Harry, so I figured they were members of his family.

We sat on a tufted leather sofa with gorgeous scrolled arms.

Harry wrung his hands and looked around the room, obviously distracted. "Are you sure I can't offer you some libation?"

"No, Harry." Best get down to it. "I came about tomorrow morning. I was hoping you wouldn't mind if I tagged along with you, you know, to the arraignment proceedings? I want to be there for him, but I just don't think I can do it alone."

I had thought about what I wanted to say to him as I walked all the way from the main building to the boathouse for the cart. I didn't want it to appear as if I was doing this because I thought he was too wimpy to handle it. And even though Fabrizio had alluded to that very thing, I had to admit going with Harry would provide me some comfort too. That is, if things went badly.

Something flickered in his eyes. Relief? Gratitude? He gently laid his hand on mine. "Why, Miss Hamilton, you don't even have to ask. It would be my pleasure to accompany you to court tomorrow."

I patted his hand with my free one. "Thank you, Mr.—"

"Harry, please."

"Thank you, Harry. I've just been so worried about Fabrizio. Having someone else there who cares about him..."

"And we both do, don't we, Miss Hamilton? Care about Fabrizio, that is."

"Yes," I said. "But I still have high hopes that we can get Fabrizio a get out of jail free card before he's formally charged."

His eyes lit up, and he smoothed his moustache, the first I'd seen of the old Harry. "Have you been successful in your discovery, Miss Hamilton, you and Mr. Stockton?"

"Well, honestly, no. Not yet. But we're still hopeful."

"Hmm, I see." He stood. "I've only just received new information from the private sleuth I hired to look into the background of the Elways and Cecile Powell Elway. I haven't even had a chance to take a look at it." He stood and offered his hand. "Would you care to join me in my study, Miss Hamilton? Who knows? It's quite possible the key to solving this mystery and having our dear Fabrizio released from that horrible place will be included in what I received."

We walked together back through the foyer to his study across from the main parlor. The walls were a rich British racing green with library prints of hunting scenes, a few illustrated maps, a huge oil painting of a brown and white foxhound—all the pieces along the wall were warmly lit by strategically placed brass art lights above each piece. Along one wall an overstuffed sofa and wing chair nestled around a serving chest with a tray of glasses and decanters. On the other side of the room, a custom-made built-in desk from the antebellum era dominated the room. It was positioned so it butted up next to a wall of bookcases and shelves. Two old-fashioned wooden office chairs positioned on either side of the two-sided kneehole told me that this wasn't only Harry's study, it was Fabrizio's study too. These two men cared so much for each other they obviously spent as much time together as they possibly could. They must both be suffering without the other.

Harry sat in one of the chairs and started to indicate I should sit opposite at what I supposed was Fabrizio's side of the desk, but then he hesitated, stood, and dragged a club chair from a corner. We both sat, and he pulled a large manila envelope from his top drawer, spilling its contents in front of him.

"My personal assistant printed all this out for me just a while ago from the attachment to an e-mail," Harry said. "Let's look at it together, shall we?"

There were copies of newspaper clippings and magazine articles, printouts of Theodore Elway's college transcripts, and articles relating to the history of his family's steel business.

Harry picked up a few sheets and handed them to me, and then he picked up the next one and began to give me a *Reader's Digest* version. "This is a short report relating to Cecile Elway née Powell of the Philadelphia Powells. She was eight years younger than Theodore and met him at a polo match about eight years after he lost his first wife. The two women could have been sisters, and Theodore was drawn to her right away.

Theodore was Cecile's second husband. Her first marriage left her well-connected socially, but unfortunately penniless." Harry stroked his moustache and gave me a *c'est la vie* sort of look. "It was awfully convenient for her that Theodore was so well-heeled. Wasn't it? But, according to what my detective has learned, she was a good and faithful wife to him up until a year or two prior to his death." He scratched the end of his nose. "And then something happened. Something about...worms?"

I nodded. "Caterpillars. Alien caterpillars. I've heard they're endangered, but that remains to be seen."

He looked positively horrified. "Alien caterpillars? I can't imagine how hideous they must be."

"Oh, Mr. Villars, you have no idea." I had looked them up online several days earlier and recalled their tiny fuzzy green bodies, bulbous green heads, and creepy little faces. I shuddered.

Harry's mouth curled with distaste. "But what do caterpillars have to do with...?"

"It's a long story, Harry, but it's possible their champion, a man named Terrence Montague, could be the murderer. I just haven't been able to find any evidence to prove it yet."

I looked down at the papers Harry had handed to me and shuffled through them. "Oh," I said, "so this is what Theodore Elway looked like."

I was looking at what appeared to be a photo off some society page that had been taken at a charity ball or some such thing. A short man who looked exactly like Super Mario smiled from under a big round nose and huge moustache. Bushy eyebrows nearly obscured beady little eyes. His suit was finely made and looked to be custom, but then the man was so short and stout that anything he wore probably had to be tailored.

The woman who was with him was considerably younger, maybe in her early forties, sweetly plump and fresh-faced with soft, hazel eyes and shoulder-length brunette hair that curled in around her jaw. Theodore had his arm around her waist. She was looking up at Theodore and he down at her. Both looked to be positively crazy about each other. Who was this pretty young woman so in love she had eyes for no one else? She looked oddly familiar to me, but I couldn't place her. Didn't know her. Did I? It was probably just that she reminded me of someone I knew once, or someone I wished I'd known.

"When was this photo taken?" I handed it to Harry.

He flipped it over and read a note inscribed on the back. "Christmas, 1999. Children's Hospital Charity Gala. Theodore Elway and guest."

"Guest?" What the heck kind of detective names someone "guest?"

For the next half hour or so, we poured over the rest of the paperwork Harry's detective had sent, but it was mostly a rehash of what we already knew—except for the identity of Mr. Elway's guest at the 1999 Christmas bash. And for some reason, I couldn't get that off my mind.

Harry and I commiserated on how we were running out of time. Once formal charges were filed against Fabrizio, the Elway entourage would be free to return to Pennsylvania, and the murderer would waltz away like a contestant on *Dancing with the Stars*. If we were going to bag us a killer, we needed to boogie.

Harry let me take the copy of the photo of Elway and the mystery woman in case it turned out that I really did know her.

CHAPTER TWENTY-ONE

———

I returned the golf cart to the boathouse. Odeo wasn't around, so I left the keys and walked back to the main building.

Months ago Jack and Harry had booked Hans Ritter, the world famous magician from Dusseldorf, for the Chamber of Illusion, The Mansion's red room dedicated exclusively to all sorts of trickery and deceit.

Once the word got out, the show sold out so quickly, they decided to book a second midnight show, which also sold out.

Over the last two days, guests had arrived from all over the continent to ooh and aah about the unequalled sleight of hand of Hans Ritter, who hardly ever set foot out of his beloved motherland.

The idea had been all Jack, and the successful promotion of the event and the hotel being filled to capacity constituted a real feather in Jack's cap, and I knew he'd be there to make sure everything was ready to go.

It was awesome he was adapting so well to become exactly what this fish out of water resort needed to find its foothold in such a competitive business. Too bad the timing sucked.

I texted him to meet me outside the theater as soon as he could take a break, and then I texted Cat, who I knew had back-to-back readings all day. Under normal circumstances, I'd have been booked all day too, but seeing as how Harry knew I was doing my darnedest to prove Fabrizio innocent, my schedule had been wiped until Tuesday morning. My tip jar would be pretty anemic by the end of the week, and the restoration fund at St.

Antoine's Parish would come up on the short end, but the way I looked at it, this was for a good cause too.

Jack walked out of the Chamber of Illusion at about ten after six. I was sitting at a table in the bar in front of the magicians' theater. It was a gorgeous custom-built oak minibar and backbar just outside the theater. The hope was that while waiting in line for the shows to begin, or during intermission, folks would queue up elbow to elbow along the marble-topped bar for a glass of wine or maybe a mint julep or Irish coffee to bring in a little extra pocket change to pay the pricey magicians Jack and Harry planned to bring to Mystic Isle.

The bar itself was an attraction—elaborately carved bar, backbar, and lighted bridge were oak. A polished brass rail was positioned just right for guests to prop up one foot, Old West–style. A dozen or so café tables were set around. The floors were hardwood, stained rich and dark. The lighting was dim except for directly over the bar, which was lit by canned lights on the bridge.

It was cozy and comfortable. I'd been there before for cocktails at a couple of other shows.

Jack wore—oh my *GQ* goodness—a tux and black tie with total aplomb, like he was born in one, displaying casual confidence the likes of Clooney. I hadn't changed from my skirt and blouse I'd worn to Harry's and felt a little dowdy in his dazzling presence.

Jack's smile was warm, his gaze warmer. "Mel." My one-syllable nickname sounded so sexy on his lips.

Cat showed up just then, so there wasn't time to bask in the spicy glow of Cap'n Jack's attention. I laid the photo of Theodore on the table, and they both leaned over for a look at it.

I explained the details Harry had given me.

"Hmm," Jack said, looking at it. "So that's Theodore. And who's the woman with him?"

"Well, that's the question, isn't it? I just have this itch that she's important somehow, but I just can't place her."

Cat stood up straight and stretched. "That's the psychic," she said, yawning.

It was like a bulb lit up over my head. Of course. I spun the photo around for a look at the woman's face. Add about forty pounds, a sour expression, a pair of heavy-framed eyeglasses, and chop off the hair—and there she was. Penny Devere, Cecile's psychic and Theodore's...what? From the heat evident in the look passing between them, she was more than his psychic adviser. What had Billy said? That Penny was Theodore's psychic adviser before she provided that service to Cecile? Hmm, Theodore and Penny? Who would've thought, and what would you call that, a psychic adviser with benefits?

I took another look. She certainly had changed. The woman in the photo was lovely and sweet and happy. Penny was frumpy and sullen and miserable. And, from all appearances, she was hot to trot for old Theodore "Super Mario" Elway.

"Holy crawdaddies," I said. "Could she? Would she? Did she?"

Cat nodded, her eyes blazing. Jack nodded, his mouth turned up in a half smile.

"Are you guys thinking what I'm thinking?" Cat said.

"If you're thinking there's more to Penny Devere than meets the eye..." Jack began.

And I finished, "Then, yeah. We're thinking exactly what you're thinking."

Jack pulled out a chair and held it for Cat then sat down himself. "So if we're all on the same page, maybe we ought to finish this book together."

* * *

A VIP ticket was delivered to Penny's room at six thirty, plenty of time for her to dress and be ready for the magic show—especially considering the way she dressed. It included a meet-and-greet champagne interlude with Hans himself. It was a very cool offering I might not even have been able to pass up, so we had high hopes Penny would show up for her special evening, which was scheduled to begin at seven thirty.

And, holy Sherlock Holmes, she did, all dolled up— well, sort of, with a sparkly barrette holding back her lifeless hair, pink lipstick you'd have expected to see on a thirteen-year-old, and I think it might have been the same dress she had on in that old photo. Regardless, she was ready-freddy for her magical connection.

Hans was a staunch supporter of anyone and everyone in the magical realm and was more than willing to help us if it meant a get out of jail free card for Fabrizio.

Hans, the Aryan boy wonder, was a tall man with pale skin and a head of blond hair more like a lion's mane than anything else. He met Penny at the stage door, his blue eyes and enormous white teeth flashing brightly. A la Elvis, he wore a black-and-gold leather jumpsuit. It fit so close to his skin it occurred to me his costume was part of his act—you know, get the audience to look anywhere and everywhere but your hands?

He swept one arm before him as he bowed low, holding her hand and then bringing it to his lips. She giggled like an adolescent at a One Direction concert. One arm snaked behind her to encircle her waist as he spoke to her in his exotic, clipped accent. "*Mein Liebling*, let me show you all the wonders of me."

Another titter from Penny as she nearly swooned.

Jack stepped beside Hans. "Miss Devere, we're so happy you could accept our invitation. We're pleased to be able to present the magic of Hans Ritter tonight."

Hans and Jack shook hands then Jack turned away. "Enjoy yourself, Miss Devere."

Hans and Penny went backstage. I couldn't help my curiosity as to exactly how showing her the "wonders" of him would be accomplished. But there was no time for that now.

Jack walked back to the table where Cat and I waited, his arms folded before him.

"Well?" I asked.

He beamed and opened his arms, revealing a cell phone in his hand.

"You got it!" I couldn't help it. I was squealing.

He activated the screen, and Cat and I leaned in to see.

The password screen popped open, and we all pretty much deflated. It was password locked.

Crappola.

But once more, it was Cat to the rescue. "Try T-H-E-O," she said.

Jack entered the corresponding letter/numbers. Lo and behold, the home screen opened. *I'm telling you, sometimes that girl scares me.*

The first part of our plan had been to get Penny's phone, which Hans, that sly devil, had handily done while charming her.

Now that the phone was open, we could read any suspicious texts or e-mails, check her contacts and...

Crappola, again. Nothing. Nothing out of the ordinary, anyway.

"Ah, hell." Jack laid the phone on the table like it had burned him. He turned away and put a hand to his forehead. "I'll never be able to unsee that."

Cat and I looked at each other. I snatched up the phone to see what had him so upset.

It was probably one of the most unfortunate things I'd ever laid eyes on.

In her photo gallery were videos. The quality was poor, jerky, and I had the impression they were quite old, maybe even shot with a legit video camera and then transferred from a computer to her phone. Theodore Elway and a younger Penny Devere. The unfortunate part was their state of undress and Twister-like positions. One video after another, and each one more imaginative than the one before it.

They had been quite the adventurers.

Cat and I looked at each other again. I laid the phone facedown on the table. She picked it back up, tilting her head to one side.

"That one looks like fun," she said. "I might try that with Q."

"TMI, Cat," I said.

"Definitely," Jack said.

Jack had been right in the first place. You just couldn't unsee that.

But one thing was for sure—Theodore and Penny had participated in one very hot and very heavy affair. I guessed that maybe Cecile Powell, who came along looking like Elway's first wife, was the reason it came to an end.

And therein lay excellent motive.

* * *

Part two of our plan was put in motion as Cat and I headed upstairs to Penny's room. While she was occupied by the magical wonders of Hans Ritter, the two of us had it in mind to "toss her room," as Cat had said. *I swear that girl's spending way too much time with Deputy Quincy.* "Toss her room?" Really?

But in the end, that was sort of what we did.

Penny's room was on the third floor, which had originally been the attic of the main plantation house. The rooms up there were quaint, cozy, mostly singles.

Jack had supplied us with a room key. I could only hope the Great Fabrizio mission didn't come back to somehow bite him in the butt. He was brave to break so many rules. The saving grace was that I had no doubt Harry Villars would stand behind him.

Cat took the closet and bathroom. I took the chest of drawers. We got lucky early on. Penny's suitcase was sitting just inside the closet, and it was locked with a small combination lock.

Cat hefted it onto the luggage rack. We were both breathing hard. This espionage stuff was fairly nerve-racking, and we stared at another lock, which meant another unlocking code.

"Use the same letter/number combination to make up T-H-E-O," Cat said. And I bent to obey.

The lock popped open, and I unzipped the bag and lifted the lid, but the thing was empty.

What a disappointment. I turned away, but Cat stood staring down into the empty bag.

She bent and began to run her hands around the edges.

"It's empty, Cat."

"Maybe it is, and maybe it isn't." She unzipped a side pocket. "I mean, why would you lock an empty bag?"

"Oh. Good point."

She reached into the pocket and pulled out a packet of envelopes bound together with a red satin ribbon. Triumphantly, she held them up for me to admire. "Because this one wasn't empty."

She handed them to me. I could hardly breathe. I'd never make a good CIA agent. My hands were shaking. She gave me a funny look and took them back. "Geez, Mel, nervous much?"

Deftly, she pulled one end of the bow, and the ribbon fell away.

The envelope was dirty as if it had been handled a lot. There was a canceled stamp in one corner and a return address—Elway Steel, with a post-office box in Philadelphia—on the opposite corner. It was addressed to Ms. Penelope Devere.

We opened it and removed a piece of trifolded corporate stationary. The letter was typewritten.

I scanned it and looked up at Cat. Only seconds later, she looked up at me. We stared into each other's eyes.

"Oh my goodness." Cat's voice was pained. "It's a *Dear Penny* letter. On corporate stationary? Who does that?"

I nodded. "And look." I pointed to the signature. "Theodore Elway followed with a slash and the initials EJ? The bastard didn't even sign the thing himself. The louse had his secretary send her an *I'm dumping you* letter."

The following letters seemed to be just as harsh and just as final. They were probably written in answer to Penny's (allegedly desperate) pleas to reconsider and take her back. Theodore explained to her in a mean-spirited manner that a man such as he had to think of the family name and stature and that Cecile Powell came from an old Philadelphia family that could trace its roots back to the Mayflower. He mentioned he doubted that Penny could trace her family history back any further than Skid Row. Nice guy, eh?

We had just begun a third letter when my cell vibrated. Text message.

From Jack.

Show ended early. She's heading your way.

Yikes!

* * *

The supply closet across the hall from Penny's room was small and stuffy and smelled of furniture polish. Through the crack I left in the door, I saw Penny steamrolling up the hall toward her room. She unlocked the door and went inside, while I settled down for my first stakeout.

After Cat and I bustled around putting everything back the way we found it, except for the kiss-off letters, Cat took the letters and headed back downstairs to give the letters to Jack. The plan was for Jack and Harry to support us with what had been discovered about Penny so far and to get Quincy on board. Cat would call him when she was back downstairs.

My job was to keep an eye on Miss Psychic Killer to make sure she didn't bring harm to anyone else before an arrest could be made.

My back hurt. I'd begun to sweat. And now I had to pee. This detective gig wasn't for wimps.

I checked the time on my phone. Just after eleven thirty. I'd been in the supply closet for over an hour.

Penny's door opened. Uh-oh. Show time.

She stuck her head out and checked both ways before opening it wider and stepping out into the empty hallway.

Was that even her? What in the name of Jean Lafitte was she wearing?

It was grey. I mean, really grey, and just the one shade of grey. It hung on her in tatters like it had been shredded by time and decay. Something really gross sat on top of her head. It appeared to be the face of a ghoul with patchy cobweb hair.

And then it hit me. It *was* the face of a ghoul, a mask, and this was Cecile's ghost, or what Rosalyn believed was Cecile's ghost.

Everything started to tumble around inside my head like clothes in a dryer, round and round, shifting and somersaulting, and what ended up on top was a revelation—what Billy said about Penny's relationship with his grandfather before he even met Cecile, what Rosalyn believed about her stepmother's involvement in Theodore's death after she took up with the caterpillar man, what Penny said about Rosalyn having been considered a little wonky in the head, the explicit selfies on the phone, the Dear Penny letters, the Halloween dress-up—it was Penny Devere, the psychic. Penny who murdered Cecile to get back at her for stealing her man and maybe for killing him, Penny who was haunting Rosalyn to have her declared incompetent so she could get her hands on the trust, probably even Penny who stole the hundred grand.

I waited for her to move a ways down the hall before stepping out of the supply closet and following her.

CHAPTER TWENTY-TWO

———

On the fly, I put my phone in silent mode and texted Jack and Cat. Neither had answered by the time Penny approached the bookcase at the end of the hall where she stopped and looked around suspiciously. I jerked to a stop at the corner and eased back. Penny turned back to the bookcase and pushed on the left side. I clamped my hand over my mouth to keep her from hearing my gasp as the right side of the bookcase swung out to reveal a dark passage directly behind it.

Holy secret passage, Batman! How'd she know about that?

Oh, yeah. She took the tour. I was going to have to do that one of these days. There was obviously more about The Mansion at Mystic Isle than met the eye.

She went through and pulled it closed behind her.

I began to squirm. What now? I glanced down at my phone. *Jack? Cat? Where the heck are you guys?*

From directly across the hall, the Villars family's grandfather clock suddenly began to clang loudly, scaring me half out of my shoes. Midnight. The witching hour? *That's what they say, anyway.* I was carried back to stormy nights when Grandmama Ida would make my hair curl with tales of haunted cemeteries and swamp monsters. That didn't seem to be the case here. My ghoul was flesh and blood, not ectoplasm and cobwebs. And for some reason that scared me even more than the other kind. Penny had already killed once, so she had little to lose if I backed her into a corner.

If the clock was striking midnight, Hans Ritter's second show of the night had just begun. That was why I hadn't heard from Jack. He was part of the show, tied up, maybe literally, or maybe even being sawed in half by now. But what about Cat? I could only hope she'd gotten my text and was rounding up a posse to come and help me catch this killer.

Chicken-livered or not, I had to move. Penny was somewhere in The Mansion—dressed to kill? I sucked it up and headed for the bookcase.

I waited a minute or two, unsure if enough time had passed since Penny went through to mask my own entry. There wasn't really any way to know, so I leaned against the left of the bookcase as Penny had done, and when the bookcase swung aside, I stepped in.

I just stood there looking around. After about a half minute, the dang bookcase swung shut all on its own. *OMG! Knock it off, Melanie. It's not haunted. Not! It's probably on a timer or something.*

I've been in caves on moonless nights that were brighter than it was in there. No way I'd make any progress without falling down and breaking a leg unless I had something to light my way. Ah, yes. Smartphone.

I pulled it from my skirt pocket and activated the flashlight, holding my breath, waiting for Penny to jump me. When she didn't, I inched forward.

The secret passage must not have been as big a secret as I initially thought. It appeared to be finished inside, walls painted, floor tiled. It could possibly be used by staff to move between floors. Hmm. Who knew?

Obviously Penny did.

Curving—maybe three, three and a half feet wide—a gradual downward slant. The light from my phone went ahead of me about ten feet and gave me some sense of safety at least as far as the next bend. I found myself holding my breath, waiting for…for what? I wasn't really sure, but I didn't have to wait long for it to happen.

Where I initially went in was just that one opening at the bookcase, and for quite a distance into the corridor I saw no other openings, and then there was one, an actual door, then another, and…

The third doorway flew open, and Penny, still in the ghostly garb, jumped me.

She must have had about fifty pounds on me, chunky monkey that she was, and she hit me like Jennifer Grey on the fly at the end of *Dirty Dancing*, sending me straight to the floor. Her anger gave her an edge and momentum, and while I was down she thwacked me on the head. I threw up my arms to ward her off. With a second blow she sent my phone flying. The light went out, and we were in complete and utter darkness. I couldn't see her, but she couldn't see me either. I rolled out and away from her, got my feet under me, and began to go hand over hand down the hall, using the walls to guide me.

She was right behind me, huffing and puffing like an old locomotive. "Give it up, Melanie," Penny wheezed. "You can run, but you can't hide."

Really? Cliché, much? There was nothing else to do but throw back at her, "Are *you* talking to *me*?" I didn't wait around for her next gem.

My hand closed on a doorknob, but it wouldn't turn. The door was locked. I moved on, rushing now. By the sound of her breathing, she was closing in on me. And to use another tired but fitting line, "I'm a lover, not a fighter."

Two more doors failed to open, and then there weren't any more. I wished I could see. I wished I could just turn and flat out run. I wished I was in Philadelphia.

In about another thirty or so feet, I sensed a change in the passageway. Cooler air came at me from more than one direction. I came to a corner and went around it. But for some reason I stopped, turned around, and went back. Crossing the hall, my hands stretched out in front of me, I felt for the opposite wall, which never materialized. The corridor had branched out, and I seemed to be standing at a crossroads. From the way air circulated around me, I had the impression I could go straight ahead, right, or left.

I chose to go left, having absolutely no idea where I was in the hotel except I was pretty sure I'd made it down to the ground floor. I came to several more doors, but again, none would open. It would likely take a service key to enter or exit from this hidden hallway, which made me wonder how Penny had managed to get around so well.

And speaking of Penny, where the heck was she? I hadn't heard her bellows-like wheeze for a minute or two. I stopped and listened for it, but instead the sound of muted laughter and applause drifted along the hallway until it reached me. Drum rolls. More applause. Oh, thank God! The magic show. It drew me up the hall, my feet less careful than before, adrenaline coursing through me. The door was suddenly before me. I put my hand on the knob and turned it. But, no. Nothing. It was locked. Just like the others. From behind me came the unmistakable thump of heavy feet at a run, and a light bobbed up and down growing closer and closer. No wonder I hadn't heard her for a while. The bitch went back upstairs and found my phone!

The light hit me, and I began to pound on the door, yelling at the top of my lungs. "Help! Help me, please. Jack! Anyone! I'm here, I'm—oof."

She hit me like a linebacker, about hip high, and carried me away from the door and down, once again, onto the floor. I was gonna be black-and-blue in the morning, if I lived to count the bruises, that is.

She got astride me and sat up. My phone landed beside me, the light eerily illuminating Penny's wild-eyed hatred and ratty tendrils of fake hair writhing around her face like Medusa's snakes. That alone was terrifying. She held my throat with her left hand, and as she raised the right one, I saw the silhouette of the gun she was holding.

Had to do something. Had to do it now, or Harry would be looking for a new tattoo artist, Cat a new roommate, and Jack? No. We hadn't even really begun to know what we were to each other.

I couldn't breathe. Couldn't think. My bladder tightened. My heart felt like it would explode right out of my chest.

The quiet voice in my head seemed to come from nowhere. "Mellie gal, you gots to move." Then it screamed, "*Now!*"

And without even thinking about it, I swung one arm while I bucked. My fist connected with the side of her head, and my hips threw her off me. The gun flew out of her hand as she was tossed aside and onto the floor.

I twisted and rolled, pulled my feet up, and was off like a sprinter out of the starting blocks. The voice in my head led me along without a light or anything to guide me, just the soft sound of the voice, "Go. Go. Go."

Then. "Left. Left." Then. "Stop. Here."

The doorknob seemed to find my hand rather than the other way around. I gripped it and twisted. It turned, and the door swung open.

CHAPTER TWENTY-THREE

———

I was standing in the indoor pool area. The soft lighting cast an ethereal glow over the lovely old structure. It was all dark blue and gold tile throughout the deck area and pool itself. I always thought of it as a lagoon setting for a *1001 Arabian Nights* and wouldn't have been surprised to see Scheherazade shimmy around the corner.

But no time for that just then. Had to move. Had to move now. Had to move fast.

But I wasn't fast enough. Before I even made it halfway around the pool, her voice stopped me cold.

"I have a gun."

I stopped. You would too.

"Turn around."

I did, and she was right. She did have a gun, and it was pointed at me. Something I'd never seen before and never really thought I would see. But here it was, and what was I going to do about it?

"You don't want to do this, Penny." But she obviously did.

She looked ridiculous standing there in her shabby ghoul garb and that nasty wig, but I didn't dare take her any way except seriously.

"I don't blame you for killing Cecile, you know." I tried to make my voice as conversational as possible. "She had it coming."

She nodded. "You don't know the half of it. She was my friend, you know. Before she knew Theo, she knew me. We went to meetings of the International Paranormal Society together. She was elected president—I was vice-president. For a while it was fun until she got lazy and started handing all the work off to me. Like a fool, I did everything she asked, and I did a hell of a job, too. She took the credit. I didn't mind so much at first because I figured eventually she'd get bored with it like she did with everything else. But not only didn't she step aside so I could run for president, she ran for another term and then another."

She paused. I waited. When she didn't go on, my brain went on overdrive trying to come up with something to keep her talking until I could think of a way out of this mess.

She took a couple of steps closer to me. "I'd been with my Theo for a couple of years. He loved me, you know, even if we couldn't tell the world. He wanted to marry me, but because of his business partners and their uppity ways, he had to wait until the timing was just right."

I nodded, sympathetically I hoped, although I felt more like a bobblehead standing there.

"Theo, he told everyone I was his psychic business adviser. That way no one thought anything about my being invited along on business trips and social gatherings."

"Makes sense to me."

Her jaw clenched, and her eyes hardened. "Then along came Cecile. She seduced him. He would never have fallen for a piece of trash like her unless she got on her knees for him. She took him from me." She screwed up her face and squeezed out a few tears. "And then the bitch killed him."

"Really? I mean, I know Rosalyn always believed that, Penny. But you believe it too?"

"I *know* it. She was all hot and bothered over that sleazy scam artist Terrence and his freaking caterpillars. Theo was onto them. You can't give away as much money as she was doling out to that charlatan and have it go unnoticed. Theo was going to put a stop to it all. He was, and he was going to come back to me. We would have been together, but no. Cecile had to have it all, and she convinced my poor darling if he were better in bed, she'd leave the caterpillar man and belong only to him. My poor, foolish love. He took the blue pills. She knew his heart wouldn't take it. She knew it. Rosalyn was right, has been right all along. If Theo couldn't get to his nitroglycerin tablets, it was because she withheld them from him. She killed him." She heaved and sobbed. Dry. Racking. But no tears.

I swallowed hard. Such grief. Such pain and rage. "So you killed her to avenge Theodore."

"He was the only man I ever loved. The only man I ever will. If not for her, we'd be living in wedded bliss today."

Unless the *timing* was never quite right. But I didn't say that. Instead, I dared to ask, "I understand why you killed her. You had to. It was as simple as that. And I have to say, it was downright brilliant."

She smiled, but it was creepy, manic. "It was too easy. Cecile wasn't a killer, not really. She couldn't handle it. Guilt was eating her alive. It was easy. I just told her that Theo's poor spirit was wandering eternally restless, crying in the dark, and if she came here and had this Fabrizio medium—I read an article about him and this resort in the Society newsletter—conjure a proper séance, his spirit could finally be at peace. She bought it, the idiot, and convincing her he wanted the clams on the half shell at the séance was nothing." Her eyes lit up as if she suddenly thought of something. "Did you know the resort tours are a gold mine of information? We learned where the cold storage is and when the kitchen staff goes on break."

"But how did you know Cecile would eat the clams?"

"I told her to, that's how. Told her that was part of my dream, part of Theodore's conditions for the séance. She had to eat the clams. She really was a simpleton, you know."

"So once you arrived, she requested the clams. You learned how to get to them by taking the guided tour of the resort. You snuck into the kitchen and tainted the clams, and dere ya go." I adopted Quincy's thick accent. "She dead."

"Yes. She was dead." She just stood there, somewhat triumphant. "The tour guide also took us through a few of those hidden passages throughout the place that were used by slaves to move about the main house without bothering the sanctity of the plantation family. It was easy to lift a master key off a housekeeper's cart. That's how I got to Rosalyn." She snorted. "Even scared the living crap out of you that one night, didn't I?"

Well, I wouldn't say that, and I didn't. "What was the purpose of haunting Rosalyn, anyway?"

She rolled her eyes and took a few more steps, which brought her to within an arm's length of me. "What are you, stupid? Cecile changed the terms for the administration of the family trust. In the event Rosalyn was unable to serve as executor, I was to be the person in charge." She laughed. "Played right into my hands, didn't she? And Theo's. You know, Theo would have wanted it this way. I wasn't going to hurt Rosalyn, not really. Theo wouldn't want that. But I could drive her crazy—just a little. No harm in that. Just enough to have her committed. Then I'd be right where I should have been all along. The mistress of the Theodore Elway legacy. As I should be."

Okay, so her sanity was out there floating around the cosmos somewhere.

"I didn't want to kill anyone else. Just Cecile, but now I have to get rid of you too."

"You don't have to. I won't—"

"Tell anyone? Sure. If you hadn't stuck your busy little nose into it to begin with, I wouldn't have to do it. I would have gotten away clean."

"Let's think about this. Let's figure out a way to—"

"The tour guide showed us the passages that are no longer used for servicing the resort. No one will hear the gunshot. By the time they find you, I'll be long gone, and no one will be any the wiser. The medium, your friend Fabrizio, will be convicted of killing Cecile. Rosalyn will be committed. And I'll—"

"You'll skate free with your ninety thousand in cash and authority over the Elway estate." Why didn't Jack come? Or Cat? Or Quincy? Where was everyone? The answer was simple. They were all at the dang magic show, and if I didn't think of something fast, I was going to be deader than Baron Samedi.

"*My* ninety thousand? What the hell are you talking about?" The look on her face was puzzled. "Never mind. It doesn't matter." She reached out with her free hand and grabbed my arm. "Now come on."

"In your dreams." I wrenched free, grabbed her arm, and twisted. She lurched at me, and we toppled sideways into the pool.

She wound up on top, bigger than I, and heavier, as the masses of material in the costume wrapped around both our legs, pulling us down. I sensed that she let go of the gun, because both her hands were suddenly in my hair, using my head to push against in a futile effort to stay afloat.

I took in a huge breath when I could and held it while she thrashed above me. I kicked free of her, let myself float down under the water, and then pushed against the bottom of the pool, brought my feet under me, and put them down. I stood erect, the water hitting me chest high. We were in the shallow end, but Penny didn't seem to be aware of that.

She screamed and gurgled and kicked and flailed. I wasn't going to be the one to tell her to stand up. I saw the gun lying at the bottom, so I took in a breath and dove down to get it. When I came back up, Jack was racing across the deck.

He dove in and swam straight to me, threw his arm around me, and pulled me to the side. He looked at me like he'd never seen me before. "You okay?"

Still out of breath from my exertions and excitement, I nodded. "Go get her," I said.

He swam back and tried to manage Penny, but in all her craziness she knocked him off his feet and rolled over onto him. The bitch was drowning my Cap'n Jack.

"Not in this world, woman."

I swam over to them and punched her in the face. She went still.

Jack grinned, wrapped his arm around her, and took her across the pool to the steps. I went too and helped him pull her up onto the top step so her head was out of the water. She wasn't a lightweight to start with, and she had all that wet fabric around her. It was like pulling a limp walrus from the water.

We huffed and puffed and finally got her far enough out of the water that she wouldn't drown.

Jack leaned back against the edge of the pool. So much for that tux, but if you were going to be rescued, a dream of a man wearing a tux straight off Fifth Avenue wasn't a bad way to go. He pushed his hair out of his eyes.

"Thanks," he said.

"No." I couldn't take my eyes off his beautiful mouth. "Thank you."

Then, out of a clear blue sky, he put one hand behind my neck and pulled me to him, planting his luscious wet lips against mine. I dissolved into a thousand brilliant sparkling stars. Ah, yes, Cap'n Jack. Every time I kissed him, it was better than the time before.

*   *   *

Quincy responded to Cat's summons at about twelve forty-five that night. He'd been out on another call and couldn't come straight there, but in the end, who needed him? I had my own tuxedoed buccaneer who managed to save the day with swashbuckling flair.

Between Jack, Lurch, and me, we managed to keep Penny corralled in Jack's office until Quincy and two other deputies came, Mirandized her, and took her statement.

I couldn't say whether or not Penny Devere was psychic, but she might have been, and maybe she saw that in the end they'd get her anyway, because she confessed to everything except stealing the money.

The two deputies cuffed her, tucked her into the back of a squad car, and took her to jail.

Two more deputies and a forensics officer from New Orleans PD arrived.

Penny's room, all her things still inside, was thoroughly tossed. It took over two hours. They found traces of the insecticide used to lace the clams on a pair of latex surgical gloves tucked into a jacket pocket. In the secret passage she and I had chased each other through earlier, they came across taloned rubber gloves and her cell phone with a horrible screeching ringtone that Rosalyn identified as the sound her spectral visitor had made. What they didn't find was the ninety thousand dollars in missing cash.

Billy, Rosalyn, and Terrence were rousted from bed to be interviewed by Q and the other deputies. They were questioned at length as to what they knew of Penny Devere.

I wasn't present at the interviews, but Quincy sat down with the three of us and gave us the *Reader's Digest* version.

Rosalyn had felt completely vindicated in her dislike of the woman and was convinced Penny's actions supported her convictions that Cecile had murdered her father.

Terrence had little to add. His only contribution had been that Cecile had, in fact, believed in Penny's psychic ability and had taken everything she said to heart, which it seemed had ultimately led to her demise.

Billy had only reiterated what he told me about Penny having been somewhat of a business adviser to his grandfather and a friend and adviser of his stepgrandmother. Guess the young man didn't know anything about all the sordid goings-on between the older generation. Just as well. All he really had to add to the scenario, according to Quincy anyway, was, "Radical, dude."

Jack, Cat, and I had taken coffee out to the front veranda hoping the caffeine would help us all keep our eyes open until all this hullaballoo was finished. It was after eight when Harry Villars drove up in his big old cream-colored '72 Benz with Fabrizio beside him.

I jumped up and ran to meet them.

"Oh, my goodness gracious, Fabrizio. I'm so glad to see you." I threw my arms around him and buried my face in his chest to keep him from seeing my tears.

"Dearest Melanie, hush. I'm here. All is well."

Quincy walked up. "Well, maybe not all."

Really? What now?

"There's still the matter of a hundred thousand dollars. And no one but Fabrizio to accuse of its theft."

I just couldn't take it anymore. I whirled around. "Damn you, Quincy Boudreaux. What the devil is wrong with you anyway? Didn't your mama teach you anything? You're never supposed to spoil a tender moment like this with crappy news. Now go away!"

He had the grace to look contrite. "I can't do that, Mel. Somebody took the money, and unless we find out who, Fabrizio's still on the hook for it."

Jack and Cat walked up, and from the look on Cat's face, I thought she might launch a screeching assault on her boyfriend, too.

The Mansion shuttle bus arrived. To put distance from the argument, we all turned and watched as Lurch rolled out a luggage cart and began to stow bags in the bus.

When he was done, he took a selfie in front of the bus then rolled the cart back to the building as several guests, including Rosalyn Whitlock, her son, Billy, and Terrence the Caterpillar Man, came out.

Lurch had taken up his normal position outside the door. Terrence stopped, spoke to Lurch, and handed him a wrapped package the size of a shoebox. They were too far away to hear what was being said. Lurch nodded slowly while Terrence turned away, walked briskly to the shuttle, and with a chipper salute in our direction, climbed aboard.

Panic began to rise in me. If I didn't do something quickly, the bus would leave, and all my suspects would slip away, and with them would go any chance Quincy had to solve the theft of the money and absolve Fabrizio of it.

"Q, can't you make them stay?" I asked. "One of them took the money. Can't you—"

He shook his head and shrugged. "No probable cause."

A low roll of thunder broke into the conversation. We paused, and all six of us looked up, but there wasn't a cloud in the sky.

Another low rumble, and we all turned, realizing that Lurch had walked up behind us and was grumbling. "Mr. Stockton." His voice was so low sometimes he was hard to hear, and sometimes, like now, its timbre nearly shook the ground. He held out the box Terrence had left him. "Mr. Montague wanted Federal Express pick this up, but then the bus came, and he said he couldn't wait any longer. He asked me to ship it."

Jack look confused. "Sure," he said. "Is there a problem?"

Lurch bent so he didn't tower quite as much over Jack and pointed to the shipping label attached to the box.

Jack looked up at Lurch, his brows drawn together. Lurch jabbed his fingers at the label a second time. Jack read,

"Ship to Mr. Terrence Montague, Hotel Royale, Buenos Aires, Argentina? Sounds as if Mr. Montague is taking a vacation. After all this, I can't say as I blame the man."

Lurch made that sound again, like a bulldozer over gravel, and jabbed his finger at the label one more time.

Jack stared at the label a beat—then two—then his eyes widened as he shouted, "Stop. Deputy! Stop that man!"

* * *

As it turned out, Terrence the Caterpillar Man had indicated the value of the box's contents at—wait for it—ninety thousand dollars.

All that sneaking around and keeping quiet and maintaining a low profile, and then the fool writes a number like that on a box he's sending out of the country?

Duh. Really?

But then he probably never planned on having anyone else see it. It was a blessing the shuttle bus driver was running early that morning, or my good friend Fabrizio might still be trying to explain why he had ten thousand dollars of Cecile Elway's money and where the rest of it was.

But that wasn't necessary. When Q peeled the brown wrapping paper off the shoebox and opened it up, all those greenbacks stared back at us.

Harry gave an uncharacteristic whoop, grabbed Fabrizio, and in a move so unlike the genteel Southern man he was bred to be, smacked him right on the mouth.

Looked like things worked out in the end, after all.

EPILOGUE

———

The Sunday following all the action at The Mansion, the action was all about St. Antoine's. A paint store over in Metairie had a contractor go belly up right in the middle of a big job, and the owner had a surplus of pale-yellow paint he was willing to donate to the cause. While it wasn't exactly a heavenly color, it was bright and sunny and cheerful, and, believe me, the folks in the Holy Cross neighborhood could really use a little of all that.

A good-sized group of Magic card players was scheduled to arrive at The Mansion the next morning for a tournament, but bookings were light that weekend, and I had the day off.

Cat and I woke up early, walked over to the Café du Monde for beignets and chicory coffee. After, we chipped in together for a taxi over to the Ninth Ward. We arrived at eight thirty, in time to help spread tarps over the new pews and run tape around the windows.

Mama and Grandmama Ida showed up about ten minutes after we did. After they set up Crockpots, a couple of hot plates, and an ice chest in the half-done kitchen to keep the hot food hot and the cold food cold for lunch, both joined us in the chapel.

Grandmama and I were busy with an enormous tarp up by the vestibule. As we worked, I told her all about the excitement at The Mansion and the part I played in it. She listened, oohing and aahing in all the appropriate spots. We spread the tarp over three rows of pews before heading back for another one. We put our arms around each other as we walked. I loved my grandmama with all my heart. And I always knew she loved me too.

* * *

"Sounds like you had quite an adventure, child." She gave me a peck on the cheek. "I'm glad I didn't know anything about it until it was all over."

"I'm glad I listened to that little voice in my head that helped me out of the water, then led me through the maze of secret passages in the hotel. If I hadn't had my own common sense to lead me along, I might not have made it either time."

She didn't say anything for a while. When I bent to pull out another tarp, she stopped me by placing her hand on top of mine. "You think that was your own subconscious you heard?"

"Well, yeah." I was a little confused. "What do you think it was?"

She smiled, looking every bit like a plump cat getting ready to lick the cream off its whiskers. "I don't think, child. I know."

I waited and when she didn't continue right away, I prompted her with a tug on her hand. "All right, Grandmama, let's hear it."

"It was your granddaddy, you silly goose."

"Oh, really?"

She nodded, helped me pick up the tarp, and then turned back toward the uncovered pews. "Maybe you don't remember, but that last day, the day before he died, he made you sit down beside him for a long talk."

"I remember." He hadn't looked sick, Granddaddy Joe. He spent a lot of time on the front porch stoop in his rocker, reading the newspaper or the Bible and listening to Dixieland jazz and gospel music. I had just turned eighteen, a high school graduate at loose ends, trying to figure out who I was going to be, where I was going to go. I'd just come back from registering at Loyola University, where I planned to attend classes that fall.

"Mellie gal," he'd said. "If someday you come home and I've moved on, I want you to know that I'm not really gone. I'll always be with you, girl, whenever you need me, watching over you."

He and I sat there, him in the rocker, me on the top step. Grandmama Ida had come out and joined us, bringing a pitcher of sweet tea with her. We talked well until after the sun had gone, about all kinds of things, the weather, the music on his boom box, the awesome green beans Grandmama bought down at the green grocer and was cooking up for dinner. When Mama came home, we all ate dinner together, and then we went to our side of the house and my grandparents to theirs.

In the morning he'd gone, "moved on," as he liked to say. I missed him every day. His laugh. The way he used to take out his teeth and make them chatter at me. The stories he told me. The love of art and music he instilled in me. I never had a father to speak of. He left for parts unknown when I was just little. But Granddaddy Joe made up for that in spades. Fabrizio reminded me so much of him. I figured that was why I felt so close to my friend.

I hadn't thought about the promise he made me for years, not until today.

My grandmama is one of the few people I feel I can talk to about some of the weirdness that goes on in this world. She's a strong believer in God and Jesus, as well as some of the spookier things none of us really has an explanation for. So I know if she thinks something's a load of cow dung, it probably is.

"Grandmama, really? You think that voice I heard those times was him? Granddaddy Joe?"

She smiled that smile that told me I was a silly young girl, but a silly young girl that was well loved. "Why of course it was, child. Does your subconscious call you 'Mellie gal'?"

I grinned back at her. Now that I thought about it, no one ever called me that. No one but him. It made me feel warm. It made me feel safe. It even made me feel a little nervous.

Along about ten, the shuttle from The Mansion pulled up out front, and about twenty of my favorite people piled out. They usually brought the bus across the river via the Crescent City Connection bridge. Jack came, of course, looking cool and sexy in a pair of loose jeans that hung low on his hips, a thin white T-shirt that had seen better days, and old canvas sneakers he'd probably had since high school. His hair was a little messy, and he didn't look like he'd bothered to shave. I'd never seen him like that, and he looked adorable.

Fabrizio and Harry came, although neither was dressed for painting. Maybe they were just there to supervise and lend moral support. Valentine and some of her kitchen staff. Lurch, looking very unusual in a pair of Bermuda shorts and a tropical print shirt with huarache sandals. He reminded me of Frankenstein on vacation, only nicer looking and happier. Odeo as well as four or five others from the maintenance department. It was a good showing from Mystic Isle, and not only was Father Brian extremely grateful for their help, so was I.

When lunchtime came, we all put down our sprayers and paint brushes and headed out in back where Mama, Grandmama, and a few of the other ladies had set up an enormous potluck table. The South was well represented, with spicy Cajun food, battered and fried chicken and shrimp, rice and beans, banana cream pudding, chocolate cake, sweet tea, lemonade. You name it, I bet it was there on that table.

I sat down in one of the folding chairs trying to balance my plate on my lap and eat without creating a total disaster of spillage.

Jack came and sat beside me, and it wasn't long before just about the whole Mystic Isle group had joined us. Even Quincy, who'd shown up just in time for lunch.

It was like a family reunion.

Fabrizio looked restored. He smiled and laughed and joined in on the conversation. I got up and refilled his glass of tea.

Never having been to a séance until that disastrous night a couple of weeks ago, there was something I'd been dying to know. I bent down and whispered in his ear. "Fabrizio, at the séance? How was it done? The cold? The sound effects? And the levitating table? That was awesome!"

I pulled away and looked down at him, that face so like my grandfather's. A light came into his eyes, and the corners of his mouth turned up. He put his index finger to his lips. "Shush," he whispered.

"Was it real, Fabrizio? You can tell me."

"Apparently Mr. Elway's daughter, Rosalyn, believed it was real. She decided to pay tribute to her father and honor Cecile's bequest. Harry can breathe easier." He just shook his head, looking very mysterious. "I love you, dearest Melanie, but the Great Fabrizio can never reveal the secrets of the dark."

I sighed and gave it up, returning to sit beside Jack.

When we'd finished eating and helping pack away the foodstuff, Jack took me by the hand.

"Let's go for a walk until they get back to work."

I nodded, more than ready for a little alone time with my Cap'n Jack.

He'd been pleasant and friendly over the past week, but I'd be lying if I said I didn't expect more than that after that hot lip-lock he planted on me that night by the pool.

The sun went behind a cloud, and the air cooled, for the time being anyway. A light breeze ruffled through my hair. The birds were going crazy in the trees, but they were high enough above us that it wasn't annoying. Back at the church, Harry Connick, Jr. sang "Just the Way You Are," and Jack pulled my hand up and kissed the back of it.

We stopped walking, and he pulled me around to face him. I encircled his neck with my arms. He began to lean down, his eyes on my mouth, and I knew he was going to kiss me, so I stood on my tiptoes to make it a little easier for him.

The meeting of our mouths was just so nice, so warm, so perfect, and the longer it went the more perfect it became. I began to get that feeling inside, the one that made me squirm a little, the one that made me want him all around me, as part of me.

"Jack." When we parted, his name was on my lips.

His mouth turned up in a sweet smile. "Melanie." Apparently my name was on his lips too. "You're not like any girl I've ever known, and I want to know you better. I want to know everything about you that you'll share with me. You're so different from all those career women in New York. Their idea of a relationship is drinks and sex."

My cheeks warmed, and I had a hard time looking him in the eye. I wouldn't mind the sex either.

"But you're real and warm. Sincere and giving. I bet you have a saying in New Orleans for the kind of girl you are..." I waited. "The kind I'd like to introduce to my mother."

I caught my breath. Really? Did he really just say that? I grinned up at him. "Hmm. That's a pretty good saying, Jack, only around here they'd likely say, 'Kinda girl I'd like to take home to Mom 'n'em.'"

He grinned. "I've learned something else they say around here." He took in a breath before, "*Laissez les bon temps rouler.*" Let the good times roll. It was sexy as hell and darn near close to perfectly executed.

"Oh, my, it drives me crazy when you speak French," I said, quoting him, quite breathless at hearing my Jack *parler*. "Cap'n Jack, looks like we might make a N'awlins man out of you yet."

Chère,
If y'all want to savor some of Valentine's N'awlins cooking, try this on for size. Yum, f'true.

Valentine's Shrimp Creole

Ingredients:
6 to 8 slices bacon, diced
$\frac{1}{2}$ cup chopped sweet onion
$\frac{1}{2}$ cup chopped green onion
1½ cups chopped green bell pepper
1 cup chopped celery
1 clove minced garlic
2 (14½ ounce) cans diced tomatoes, with juice
3 Tablespoons tomato paste
$\frac{1}{2}$ cup chicken broth or stock
$\frac{1}{4}$ cup red wine vinegar
$\frac{1}{2}$ teaspoon mustard
Splash of Tabasco sauce
Salt and pepper to taste
$\frac{1}{2}$ cup dry red wine (plus some to splash in if sauce gets too thick)
1 lb large raw shrimp, peeled and deveined

Total time: about 50 minutes
(Prep: 10 minutes / Cook: 35-40 minutes)

Fry the bacon until crispy over medium-high heat in a large skillet. Set it aside, leaving 2 tablespoons bacon drippings in the skillet. Reduce heat to medium. Add the onions, bell pepper, celery, and garlic. Sauté until tender, 5-6 minutes. Add tomatoes, tomato paste, chicken broth, vinegar, mustard, Tabasco sauce, salt, and pepper. Return bacon to pan. Simmer it all over low to medium heat, uncovered, for 15-20 minutes, stirring occasionally. Add wine and shrimp, and cook until shrimp turns pink (don't overcook), about 4-5 minutes. If sauce is too thick after, splash in some red wine to desired consistency.

Serve over rice or biscuits. Makes 4 to 6 servings.

ABOUT THE AUTHORS

Sally J. Smith and Jean Steffens, are partners in crime—crime writing, that is. They live in Scottsdale, Arizona, awesome for eight months out of the year, an inferno the other four. They write bloody murder, flirty romance, and wicked humor all in one package. When their heads aren't together over a manuscript, you'll probably find them at a movie or play, a hockey game or the mall, or at one of the hundreds of places to find a great meal in the Valley of the Sun.

To learn more about Sally & Jean, visit them online at
www.smithandsteffens.com

Enjoyed this book? Check out these other novels available in print now from Gemma Halliday Publishing:

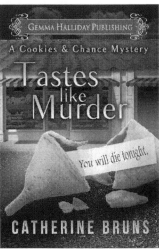

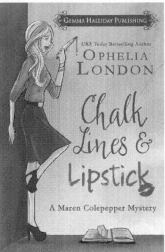

www.GemmaHallidayPublishing.com

Made in the USA
Lexington, KY
29 October 2015